Acknowledgements

Thanks to Paul Brown, Randy Lindsay, Rick Loomis, Ken St. Andre, Robert Kassebaum, Jay Sanford, Dan Fogel and Lee Kline.

Special thanks to proofers Anita, Molly Baker
& Sandy Stratton all of whom went beyond the call of duty
in helping us get this book in readable shape!

Book design & additional graphics and illustrations
by Steve Crompton.

First Edition - January 2012

D'Molay's map of the Inner Realms of the Gods.

CITY OF THE GODS
MYTHIC TALES

Stories of the Gods by
M. Scott Verne, Wynn Mercere
Ken St. Andre, Jefferson Swycaffer, Anita Martinez,
Jay Allen Sanford, Robert Kassebaum,
Randy Lindsay, Wendall Brown,
Edgar Allan Poe & Bram Stoker

RAVEN PRESS

CITY OF THE GODS: MYTHIC TALES

First Edition - January 2012

ISBN: 978-0-9836929-1-1

www.CityoftheGods.com

Published by

RAVEN PRESS
PO Box 2018, Scottsdale, AZ 85252

Contents

Welcome to the City

One day, all the gods known in story and legend left our Earth for a place of their own. In this place each pantheon of deities has its own land to command. The Norse Gods rule the Cold Lands and the Egyptian Gods rule the deserts; the Greek Gods preside over the Olympian realm, and so on. In the center of it all, on an island, is the City of the Gods, a place filled with beauty, grandeur and intrigue. The deeper questions as to why the gods left Earth, and what has happened to them since they left, are being answered in the City of the Gods novels.

This book is a perfect introduction for those who wish a glimpse into this unique realm. Readers will encounter many characters that appear in City of the Gods: Forgotten, along with other denizens of the Godly Realms. Those who have already read this first novel will learn more about key characters including D'Molay, Aavi, Mazu, Tenh-Mer, Sekhmet, Sergius, and many others. Mythic Tales is filled with swashbuckling action, romantic tragedy, humorous escapades, political drama and horror - something special for every reader.

As a tribute to classic authors who have inspired us, we've also included two "forgotten" mythical stories by Edgar Allan Poe and Bram Stoker.

We hope you will enjoy spending time in the City of the Gods and will want to visit here again.

M. Scott Verne & Wynn Mercere

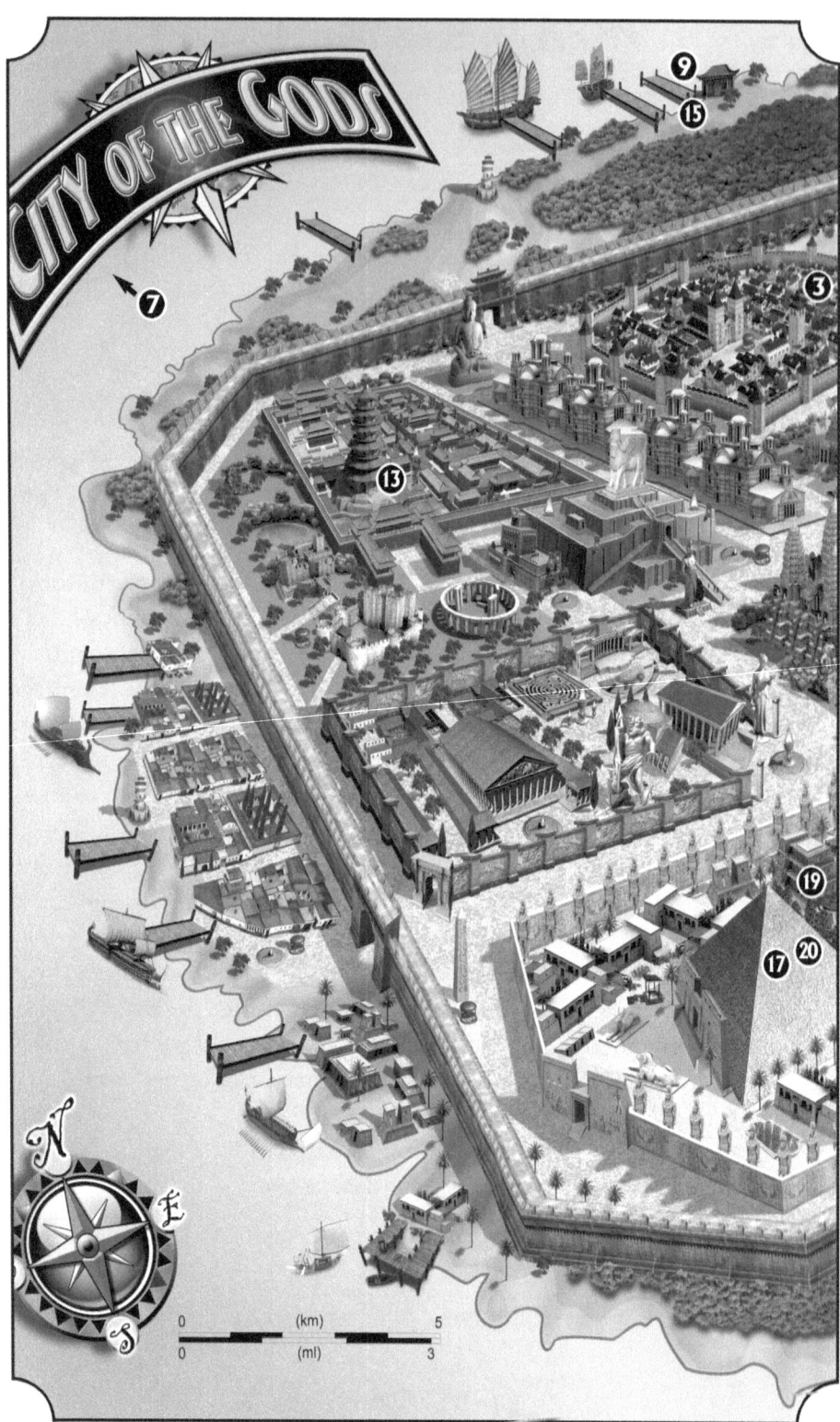

Characters From the First Book

Many characters featured in this anthology are from *City of the Gods: Forgotten*. Some of them do not live in the City, but are visitors from the outer realms of the gods. These are marked with a 'V' in the table below. Each being has a numbered location on the map (see previous 2 pages) that represents where they spend most of their time. Lastly, the chapter number designates when they first appear in *City of the Gods: Forgotten* (2nd Edition).

Map Location	Name	Visitor or Resident	Social Status	1st Novel Chapter No.
1	Anansi	V	Minor God	10
2	Aavi	V	Slave	2
3	D'Molay	R	Freeman	Prolog
4	Eros	V	God	1
5	Es-huh	R	Slave	11
6	Geirronol	R	City Guard	5
7	Glaucus	V	Minor God	13
8	Hermes	V	God	20
9	Mazu	R	Minor God	3
10	Mod, Magni, & Hod	V	Minor Gods	15
11	Mordecai	R	Slave/Guard	7
12	Namtar	R	God	7
13	Nianzu	V	Servant	4
14	Oloth	R	Slave/Guard	12
15	Quan	V	Servant	27
16	Quetzalcoatl	R	Major God	1
17	Sekhmet	R	God	5
18	Sergius	R	Freeman	20
19	Set	R	Major God	19
20	Tenh-Mer	R	Servant	5
21	Slave Girl	R	Slave	15

The Infernal Triangle

By M. Scott Verne & Wynn Mercere
Guest Illustrations by Liz Danforth

Long ago on Earth, Circe, daughter of Helios the Titan and the goddess Hecate, lived with her nymph attendants on the island of Aiaia. She was skilled in the magic of metamorphosis, the power of illusion, and the dark art of necromancy. She is best known from the saga of Odysseus, wherein she transformed Odysseus and his men into animals when they landed on her island. However, there is another often "forgotten" story that involves Circe in a love triangle between the god Glaucus and the nymph Scylla. All three of these mythical beings play a part in the first and second City of the Gods novels.

Circe set aside the sleeping powder she had compounded for Nemesis and wondered when she would come to retrieve it. Such a passing thought was a stinging reminder to Circe of just how lonely she was on her remote island. No one with any sense would look forward to a visit from the goddess of punishment, but even her appearance would be a break in Circe's routine. Almost as if her thoughts had compelled a visitor to appear. to do her bidding, a servant knocked on Circe's chamber door.

"Mistress Circe, a visitor has arrived upon our shores," a nymph announced.

"Tell Nemesis I'll be right down," she replied flatly, knowing the brief visit from the unpleasant goddess would do little to ease her own depression.

The nymph stood in front of Circe, her feet together and her hands held behind her back. She smiled broadly and even bounced a little as she delivered unexpected news. "It isn't Nemesis. It's the sea god Glaucus and he wishes to see you."

Circe leaned forward. "Glaucus? Have him wait in the lagoon while I ready myself. Well, go girl - don't just stand there grinning at me like the village idiot... Go!"

As the pixie-like girl scampered out of the chamber, Circe called after her. "Take Glaucus wine and dance for him. I'll meet him by the bathing pools!" Circe called for other attendants to come and help her dress more appropriately for the occasion. She had known Glaucus in her youth and found him quite attractive, though they had only met a few times at the court of her father. "So, he's still on Earth too," Circe thought to herself.

In short order Circe was dressed, coiffed and anointed with sweet smelling oils. Servants had moved her throne and placed it beside the bathing pool fed by the lagoon, as Glaucus could not walk upon the land. Circe positioned herself upon her chair, holding her staff in one hand and a crystal globe in the other. Nearby, one of her former lovers whom she had transformed into a mute monkey sat idly by watching her get ready. Ignoring the creature, she stared at the two objects in her hands. "No, it's too many things. Take them away. I want my hands free, ere I need to reach out to him."

As a nymph stepped forward quickly and took the items, Circe adjusted the folds of her gown. "All right, let him in." She tried to make her pose look casual, as if she were always regally dressed and sitting on her throne by the pool, waiting for suitors.

The nymphs pulled up a gate that connected the pool to the seawater and she saw the sleek, muscular form of Glaucus swim through the channel. He jumped out of the water for a brief second or two the way happy dolphins often do. He waved to Circe as he fell back into the pool, then swam to her.

Circe let out a sigh as she watched. She loved the way he moved through the water, a rhythmic dance of man and fish. She had admired him from afar from the first time she saw him when she was but a teenaged girl. Ever since that time, she had been obsessed with the idea of transforming men she liked into half beasts, subconsciously trying to recreate the unattainable man with whom she was obsessed: Glaucus

He emerged from the water, leaning up against the pools edge. "Circe! You look resplendent today. I remember you as a slip of girl and here you sit, a queenly goddess! Thank you for agreeing to see me."

Circe smiled coquettishly. "Oh Glaucus, I would always welcome your arrival on my shores. I remember well your visits to my father's court and treasure those days."

"Is he still in Greece?" Glaucus inquired politely. "I should visit, it has been a long, long time."

Circe shook her head. "Father is gone now. He rules a kingdom in the new Olympia and there is a mortal ruler in his old palace." Circe tried to keep the sadness from her voice, for she truly missed those long-gone days. But as the two of them spoke of Glaucus' visits to Helios' palace and the memories they shared, her heart warmed. They reminisced for half an hour, recalling other godly visitors to her father's court and some of the more memorable entertainments that they had seen. Finally, they caught up on what had happened to other gods they had both known. Many had left the Earth and gone to live in the new realms ruled by the City of the Gods.

Circe giggled slightly as she moved on the next subject. "So, Glaucus, this has been marvelous, but I'm sure you didn't swim all this way to reminisce about old times. Why have you come?" Circe dared to hope that he had a more personal reason to see her. Despite her efforts to remain regal and subtle, Circe was having trouble restraining her flirtatious nature and suppressing her long-term attraction for the sea god.

He hesitated. "I must confess, I know of your skills with magic and I have come to ask a favor of you, as a friend of your father," he said from the pools edge, his fish tail swaying slowly back and forth in the water.

Circe sat back to consider his statement. "A favor from me?" She placed her hand upon her bosom to emphasize her mock surprise at such a request. "Well, since you are a long-time friend of my father's I am happy to help. If your favor is within my power to grant, I will do it for you, Glaucus." Then she gave him a slow smile and a somewhat longing gaze as she waited for him to speak. Circe saw no evidence that Glaucus was noticing her overtures, but she continued to play her part until his answer shook her composure.

"I have heard you can make a spell, a potion that can make another fall in love. Is this true?"

"A - a love spell? Why would you of all people need a love spell? Surely the women must flock to you . . . so handsome, so powerful." Her voice was low, trancelike.

"Hah! Me? You jest, Circe. No woman in her right mind would want me, I'm only half a man!" He held his fish tail out of the water in emphasis.

Circe's alarm was evident from the tight grip of her hands on the chair cushions, but she managed to keep the rising distress from her voice. "That's not so! Believe me when I tell you that I know women find you quite attractive. You are unique, special. You move through the water so gracefully and you have such amazing stories to tell of what lies beneath the seas."

Glaucus looked down, chagrined. "Circe, you are kind, and I will not argue with you, for I came to ask a favor. Can you make me this potion?"

Circe battled with her emotions. The girlish part of her held hope that he was about to proclaim his love for her, that he would explain he wanted to use the potion to make her fall in love with him. Circe imagined how they would both laugh joyously when she would reveal that she didn't need a love potion for she already loved him. But a darker part of her nature seemed to sense this outcome was mere fantasy. She pushed her dreams aside and sought the truth.

"Yes... but there are things I need to know to make a love spell. Who is this potion for?"

Glaucus leaned forward eagerly. "I love a water nymph named Scylla but she has no love for me. She is all I think about, night and day. Help me, Circe, I'm desperate to - "

"Y - you fell in love with a nymph? I . . . " Circe was mortified as she felt her tears rise up. Too proud to let him see her foolish feelings, she abruptly stood. "I'll check my spell books on potions for nymphs." Quickly, she headed away from the pool and into her pavilion, tears streaming down her face, hands balled into fists. She entered a guest bedroom and fell onto the bed, crying out and pounding her fists against the mattress. Each time her fist hit the bed, a black burn mark appeared as her mystic energy flowed forth.

One of her nymphs appeared at the door. "Mistress, are you all right?" Circe rounded on her in fury.

"YOU! Your kind's seductive ways are to blame for this!" Circe pointed at the hapless nymph and a blindingly bright bolt of energy blasted the girl into ashes. Circe felt an intense satisfaction as the ashes fell to the floor in a small pile, creating the perfect ingredient for a vengeful potion.

Glaucus slowly swam circuits of the pool while a small group of the nymphs stood by Circe's throne. They had brought him food and performed for him, but now that several hours had passed, the servants merely waited with him. From time to time, one would reassure him that her Mistress would return shortly, or another would remind him that brewing potions was a slow process. He barely heard their excuses. His goal of gaining Scylla's love was in sight, and embracing her was the only thing for which he could spare a thought.

At long last Circe returned. A nymph attendant carried a sealed amphora about the size of a loaf of bread. Circe passed by her throne and dropped to her knees by the pool's edge. Glaucus swam over to her, and they faced each other, as close as they had ever been.

"I bring you your potion, Glaucus, but first hear me out, for I have something else to offer you."

Glaucus smiled. "I am so grateful for this, Circe. I need no more, but please tell me whatever you wish." His gaze broke with hers and he looked quickly at the coveted love potion. Circe quietly raged that even now she seemed unable to hold his attention. She bit back the bitter words that rose to her tongue to try one last time to win him. She reached out, touched his cheek, and turned his face back to her own.

"I know you love this Scylla, but she loves you not. A potion could change that, but it wouldn't truly be love, just a spell. Please, Glaucus, forget this girl and stay here with me. I have loved you from afar for so long, only now do I have the courage to tell you this; let me embrace you. I can offer you pleasures and joys no mere nymph could. I pray that I could be yours, Glaucus." Circe had hoped to say all this slowly and seductively, but it spilled out with speed as she was too excited to restrain herself, hopeful that he might finally realize that he loved her as well.

A look of surprise flashed over Glaucus' face, but almost instantly pity settled in. "Circe . . . I am touched by your words, I truly am, but I fear that love itself is a spell and I have been struck by the arrow of Eros. I am in love with Scylla. I can no more change that than tree leaves could grow at the bottom of the ocean or seaweed on the hills of your island. I'm so sorry." He reached out and touched her hand in offer of comfort.

Circe's eyes opened wide and she withdrew her hand. "You would spurn me for a mere nymph? All I have to offer? Can she cast spells or change the weather? Does she have an island and servants?"

"No, no, she has none of those things, but she can travel in the oceans and deep into the waters. We have traveled together, she and I, and while she does not love me, she calls me friend, and I love her. There is no more to it than that," Glaucus shrugged.

Circe stood up, her fingers curled tightly as she restrained herself from boiling the water Glaucus was in and destroying every nymph for leagues. She spoke slowly and deliberately. "I see. I have exposed my heart for nothing, then." She turned away and barked to the nymph holding the amphora. "Give him the potion."

The nymph stepped forward and held it out to Glaucus. He took it, holding it tightly to his chest as if Circe might try to take it back. "Thank you. I am truly in your debt."

She glared at him angrily. "Then do me the favor of leaving and never return here. The sight of you now brings me nothing but pain. To make the potion work, pour it into the waters near your nymph. Then she will love you, and you can be with her always. Now go! Go to your Scylla, for I am done with you." Circe turned to walk away.

"I won't forget this favor you have granted me, never," Glaucus called after her, but she did not answer.

The attendants who followed Circe heard her mutter under her breath. "No, I'm sure you won't forget it." Then she wheeled on them and ordered, "Bring me the crystal orb. It's time I call upon Zeus and tell him I wish to go see my father and mother. I've suddenly grown weary of Earth."

As they prepared to leave, Circe could not resist the urge to see how her potion worked. "Bring me the orb," she ordered the nearest nymph. Soon, Circe sat cross-legged in her bedroom, with the orb in her lap, watching Glaucus eagerly.

Glaucus sped to the shores where Scylla lived, but he did not seek her out among the rocky shoreline where she loved to watch the fish dart across the tidal pools. Instead, he watched and waited for her to return to the ocean to renew her strength in the water, something she had to do from time to time. Only then did he swim up to greet her, opening the amphora and letting its dark liquid out into the water. He tried to make it seem like a game and she laughed as the dark liquid started to swirl around her. Very quickly she was surrounded by it; then Scylla started to panic.

Glaucus could see her fear and tried to calm her. Then he realized something was going wrong, terribly wrong. Scylla writhed in pain as her entire body started to change grotesquely. Her face stretched into a toothy maw and spikes shot out from her spine. Her legs merged together and her hands became fin-like claws. Scylla grew larger and larger until she looked nothing like the nymph he had come to love. She had transformed into a hideous sea serpent right before his eyes. He screamed in pain and horror, knowing that although Circe had betrayed him, the ultimate guilt for Scylla's fate was his to bear alone.

Suddenly Scylla lashed out at him, snapping with her huge alligator jaws. Glaucus just managed to escape being bitten in half and frantically swam away to hide among the clutter of sea plants and debris that clung to the nearby shoals. He waited, eventually approaching Scylla again to see if there was anything he could do to help her, but each time he came near she would try to eat him. Later, alone and miserable, he realized that Circe had told her own version of the truth in regard to the potion; Scylla loved him, but only as a tasty morsel. And he could be with her forever, if he allowed her to eat him.

Glaucus was a broken man.

Circe watched intently as the events unfolded. For a few seconds, she felt a slight pang of pity for the pair, then she leaned back and started to laugh, a malicious grin on her face. The spell had worked perfectly.

Glaucus only hope lay in convincing Circe to undo the horrible spell. He vowed to force her, or die in the attempt. Traveling back to her island, he discovered she was gone, the island abandoned. So Scylla, trapped in the form of a hideous sea creature, continued to attack anyone who came near.

She killed many a sailor and destroyed many ships. When the time of the great leaving came, she was taken from the Earth by the gods of Olympus whose duty required them to remove any creatures their kindred had created. Where they put the creature called Scylla remains a mystery.

Glaucus too was taken up to the realms of the gods, where he remained, immortal and despondent, for he had not only lost the one person he loved, but he had destroyed her as well. He lives in a crumbling temple on a small island.

Even after she left Earth, Circe still toyed with gruff, powerful men and even fell in love with them from time to time. But again and again she tired of them, either set them free or turned them into animals. Circe continued to create potions for the gods, but for reasons unknown, she went into hiding. Like Scylla, her current whereabouts remain a mystery.

Roped In

By Wynn Mercere

*The goddess Mazu planned to leave all her companions on
Earth behind when she left for the City of the Gods.
But two of them were not content to see her go alone.*

The morning of her departure from Earth was warm and clear. Mazu sat, admiring the budding trees, with her constant companions, two great demons. They had once been famous men, brothers and accomplished generals, but when they died defeated, fate served them an afterlife in monstrous form. When Mazu first met Quanli Yan and Shunfeng Er, they confronted her with the ridiculous proposal that she marry one or both of them. To their chagrin, the goddess subdued them in battle and forced them into her service. Over the years they had become her friends, but they were a liability at times. She often regarded the demons as exuberant pet dogs - loyal, but in need of obedience training.

"You demons are so troublesome," Mazu sighed, casting a distracted glance at the far mountaintop. "I already told you I'm traveling alone. And you in turn promised to watch over the shrines and villages while I'm gone."

Quanli Yan stopped trimming his right horn, flicking a bright red shaving in the direction of his green brother, Shunfeng Er. "But we are your body guards, Mazu. Why take our main purpose away from us?" He waved his knife energetically at the goddess, hoping the many times his blade had served her well would change her mind.

Shunfeng Er brushed the red demon's horn debris from where it had landed on his sleeve. "I can see why you want to be rid of him," he said to Mazu, indicating Quanli Yan, "so I'll compromise. Leave him here to watch, but take me with you. Who knows what dangers await on that mountain?"

"What good would you be on her journey?" Quanli Yan protested. "I am General Thousand Miles Eye! I can see all the way to the top of the mountain while sitting right here. What better guard could the goddess have than that?" The red demon puffed up, striking the flat of his blade against his armored chest.

Shunfeng Er grunted. "Don't you listen? She doesn't want you. If you had the keen hearing of me, General With-the-Wind Ear, you would know this." The green demon lifted his bow, released an arrow, and the death cry of some creature previously unnoticed by the weaker senses of the others came to the ears of his companions.

Mazu gave neither of them encouragement. Nonetheless, the argument escalated into a physical confrontation. Quanli Yan jumped to his feet and demanded that Shunfeng Er prove he was the better brother. Soon they were wrestling and rolling down the gentle rise of the foothill at the mountain's base. Seeing her opportunity, Mazu rose and quickly began her trip up the mountain, unnoticed by the squabbling brothers.

Ten minutes of battling later, Quanli Yan landed a solid kick to Shunfeng Er's belly. The green demon flew through the air until a pile of fallen boulders stopped his progress. As Quanli Yan ran toward him to get in a few more kicks, Shunfeng Er held up a hand to forestall him. This action surprised Quanli Yan, for neither of them ever begged for mercy in their fights.

"Listen!" Shunfeng Er commanded. "Someone is near."

Quanli Yan tilted his head skeptically. "It's probably just Lady Mazu coming to stop our fighting." He looked back up the hillside expecting to see the goddess. He didn't. Alarmed, he cast his far-sight along the rise of the mountain trail and still saw no trace of her. His visual gifts, extraordinary as they were, could not perceive the goddess when she chose not to be seen.

Shunfeng Er got to his feet and walked over to Quanli Yan. Nudging him, he turned his brother toward the other end of the trail that led upward from a nearby shrine. "Down there. Two monks."

"They have a beautiful robe," Quanli Yan observed, able to pick out the smallest details on the bundle borne on the back of the younger monk. "And a ceremonial scroll," he added, after studying the gear of the older man. Their lips were moving, so Quanli Yan turned to Shunfeng Er and his keen ears. "What are they saying?"

"They're talking about Mazu leaving for heaven to live forever in the City of the Gods," Shunfeng Er said, surprised. "And they say she is waiting for them to arrive with that garment."

"Leaving? City of the Gods?" Quanli Yan jerked his neck in the direction of the sky above the mountain peak to try to see this place of which he'd never heard floating in the sky. "I can't see a thing. Has she really abandoned us forever?"

Shunfeng Er's heart sunk. "Would she have been so firm about making us promise to protect the shrines and the villages if that wasn't her plan?"

"Maybe you heard wrong," Quanli Yan said, words which almost started their fight anew. But he ran off in the direction of the monks before Shunfeng Er could express his offense.

The green demon hurried after him, bounding with his brother over the landscape with great speed until Quanli Yan paused by a spring at the side of the trail where travelers always stopped for a drink.

"What's your plan?" Shunfeng Er asked, knowing his brother already had one. Of the pair, he was the wisest in strategy.

"I'm going to get them to take us to Mazu in secret," Quanli Yan revealed. "Change yourself into a cord of silken rope." Shunfeng Er's mouth gaped and his brother punched him hard in the shoulder. "Just do as I say!"

A moment later the demon had shape shifted into a beautiful length of green cord with decorative knotted designs at both ends. Quanli Yan smiled, amused that Shunfeng Er still held to the stylish tastes he had when he was human. He then emptied the coins from a fine leather pouch he carried into his boot and placed the silk rope into the empty bag, shushing Shunfeng Er's grumbling with a tap on the bag as the monks came around a bend in the trail. Quanli Yan picked up a hollowed drinking gourd left by the waters and was sipping from it as the older monk greeted him.

"Red General," the monk said with a slight bow. "Is the road clear today?"

"It is. Nothing will slow your travel to meet the goddess." Quanli Yan offered the drinking gourd to the younger monk, who stepped forward to refresh himself. "She has asked my brother and I to guard these lands, otherwise we would go with you to see her off."

"The villages are in your debt," the older monk said, looking around. "Where is Green General? I would like to thank him too."

Quanli Yan shrugged, pretending not to know or care. "We fought this morning. I won. He is sulking."

The bag he held twitched as Shunfeng Er wiggled angrily at the lie, but Quanli Yan's large hand hid this from the humans.

"Master, we should hurry. The sun is almost overhead," urged the young man. His companion looked to the sky, and nodded.

"You are right. Please excuse us, General."

Quanli Yan stepped out onto the trail, blocking their way. "Before you go, I have a favor to ask of you. My brother and I have a gift for Lady Mazu. Two special belts to match the robe you bear." He held out the leather pouch and opened it slightly. Part of Shunfeng Er fell out. "One is green and one is red, to remind the goddess of her faithful generals." He tucked his brother-turned-to-rope back into the bag and tied the pouch loosely to the younger monk's pack. "But don't tell her about this. It's a surprise. There is a note inside that she can discover for herself."

"We will deliver your secret gift," the old monk promised. The holy men bowed again in farewell and continued up the trail. At their pace, they had at least a three-hour climb ahead of them, time enough for Quanli Yan to put the next part of his plan into action. The demon waited impatiently for a few minutes before climbing to the top of a tall tree. From the heights, with the gift of his enhanced vision, it was easy to watch the monks. Their path was challenging. They no longer had breath to spend the time conversing. With the old monk in the lead, the younger one dutifully followed his Master, who never looked back to check on his student. Every few minutes Quanli Yan leapt to another treetop further up the mountain, so that when the slipshod knot he had tied worked loose from the young monk's pack he was able to jump down to meet the pouch when it hit the ground. Quanli Yan landed at the mouth of the pouch and instantly transformed himself into a red rope, falling in a cascade at the opening as if he had spilled from it.

"A moment, Master," the young monk said, turning as he heard the pouch hit the ground. He stooped to gather up the leather sack and tuck the red cord inside, allowing Quanli Yan to join Shunfeng Er. Pressed together in the dark, the demons almost started to fight again, but restrained their urges for the time it took the monks to finish their trek up the mountain.

"I hear Mazu breathing," Shunfeng Er whispered at long last. "We are close." Then both of them heard the older monk greet the goddess and listened to their mistress reply.

"It's kind of you to be of one last service to me," Mazu said. "I can leave this world without worry knowing that men such as you will remain behind."

"We have brought your ceremonial robe as you asked," the older voice replied. The demons inside the pouch were jostled and heard the rustling of leather against cloth.

"So I see. Now I will be respectfully dressed in heaven. No one in the City of the Gods will be able to find fault with my splendor," Mazu said as the brothers felt the heavy robe shift some more.

"What's happening?" Shunfeng Er asked in a faint whisper.

"I think we've been put in her shoulder bag," Quanli Yan told him softly. "I can see the faint glow that comes from her vial that contains the water of life."

"Ah, you are right, then," Shunfeng Er judged, for Mazu always carried that item safely inside her pack.

"Goodbye, Compassionate Mazu," they heard the monks say in unison. Shunfeng Er heard the sound of a scroll unrolling just before the monks recited a special prayer. Then followed a thunderous rush of wind as Mazu ascended and the world receded beneath them.

Quanli Yan and Shunfeng Er could barely maintain their excitement when the sound of the whirlwind that carried Mazu was replaced by a multitude of strange chants, exotic music, and the lowing of pack animals. Mazu's body now moved in a slow walk, her shoulder bag rocking the demons gently against her hip. The brothers strained to understand the jumble of unknown languages that were being spoken. Finally, they heard someone speak to Mazu in their tongue.

"If you brought a retinue, send it to wait over there," the voice directed. "Only gods and goddesses can pass by the gate guardians at this time."

"Did you hear that? Guardians," Shunfeng Er murmured. "Maybe we're going into a fortress. We should take our true forms and show them what great generals we are."

Quanli Yan grunted his disagreement. "Not yet, unless you want to wait outside the walls with the rest of the gods' servants. We must stay as we are until Mazu is inside."

After a short pause Mazu's even steps resumed. Then she stood still for barely a moment before a high-pitched squealing noise made Shunfeng Er flinch. "An alarm!"

The shoulder bag was seized and the demons were roughly dumped from their hiding place. They landed atop one another at Mazu's feet. Quanli Yan immediately tried to change back to his true form, but he could not.

"I can't transform!" Shunfeng Er cried out, finding himself in the same situation. The demons wiggled like snakes in an attempt to flee, but were soon pinned to the ground by heavy-booted feet. Shunfeng Er looked up helplessly through his rope-knot eyes at a crystal standing stone from which shone the image of a foreign goddess. She was glaring at Mazu with an irritated expression. Quanli Yan peered up at some type of armored guard that stood on them with a deadly-looking spear held at the ready.

"I see in your heart that you have been tricked, Lady Mazu," the shimmering reflection lectured. "The trespass of your servants is not your fault. After we destroy them, you will be allowed to enter the City."

"Destroy us!" Quanli Yan shouted. "You can't do that! Release us immediately!" He blustered and writhed to no effect. Shunfeng Er tried again to escape while all attention was on his brother, but to no avail. Through it all, Mazu remained silent until the spear carried by the armored guard standing on her companions began to glow.

"Wait," she forestalled. "What if I choose not to enter the City?"

Her suggestion surprised the goddess in the crystal. "Why would you choose this?"

A new voice from behind Mazu and the demons entered the conversation. A man spoke at length. Though Quanli Yan and Shunfeng Er could not understand his language, the tone of his words was kind and persuasive. There was a likeable force and charisma in his speech that gave the demons hope.

"The god Eros of Olympia has vouched for your devious servants," the crystal image translated for Mazu. "He sees only devotion to you in their hearts. Taking his judgment into consideration, I will not have them destroyed."

"Thank you," Mazu began, but she was interrupted.

"Nonetheless, you agreed to rules when you chose to come to this world and some penalty must be paid for this irregular situation. Your minions must remain as they are for the next thousand years, and you, Mazu, must remain outside the City gates for that same time." Eros made another comment which the goddess translated, albeit with a bit of weary sarcasm in her voice. "Eros says not to despair, for the realms are a big place with enough sights to keep you entertained for twice that many years."

"Then I will go into them and be grateful for your leniency," Mazu said. Quanli Yan and Shunfeng Er quivered in relief as Mazu scooped them up and pushed back through the line of deities waiting to be judged by the crystal gate guardian.

"How we have fallen, brother," Shunfeng Er lamented lightly. "From great generals, to demons, and now this."

Mazu stepped into a less crowded spot and paused to tie her errant generals tightly around her waist. "I knew you two would cause me trouble if I let you come. I will have to think of some useful work for you two ropes to do. Perhaps I'll fish with you, or wind you around a mill stone."

"Whatever you wish, Mazu," Quanli Yan agreed. "But remember, I am the strongest, so save the harder work for me."

Shunfeng Er objected, and their fighting began anew.

Becoming the Spider God

African folktale adapted by M. Scott Verne

Becoming the Spider God

*Anansi appears in City of the Gods: Forgotten at the slave auction with
the Asian god Cai Shen. Anansi's legend originated in West Africa and was
brought to Jamaica and other parts of the New World by Ashanti slaves, the
mythic tale handed down orally through generations. Anansi exists as a spider,
a man, or a combination of the two. Anansi is no goody-two-shoes hero.
He is a greedy, lazy, inventive trickster, cunning and smart in the extreme.
Anansi loves a joke. When he's not sleeping is always up to
something, though he will help those truly in need.*

There was once an Afrik god called Chiuta who owned the finest ram
in the world. Since Chiuta ruled over all of Afrik, he did not concern
himself where his ram wandered, as all the lands were his, and all the people feared his wrath - except one.

His name was Anansi and he did not think the gods bothered with mortals. In fact, he doubted the gods ever heard the prayers of the people, for the land was dry and the rains did not come. "Surely if Chiuta truly cared for us, he would bring the rain," Anansi would tell his neighbors as he watched his crops dying in the hot sun.

One day the great ram happened to be grazing on Anansi's crops. Anansi threw a rock at it, hitting it between the eyes and killing it.

Despite his doubts about the attention gods paid to mankind's affairs, Anansi worried that Chiuta would punish him for killing the prized creature. He immediately schemed for a way out of the situation. Anansi was sitting under a tree thinking of an escape when a nut fell and struck him on the head. Anansi immediately had an idea. First, he took the dead ram and tied it to the nut tree. Then he went to a spider and told it of a wonderful tree laden with nuts.

The spider was delighted and immediately went to the tree. Anansi then prayed to Chiuta and told him that the spider had evidently killed the prize ram; the ram was hanging from a tree where the spider was spinning webs. Chiuta flew into a rage and demanded the death penalty for the spider.

Chiuta thanked Anansi and offered him a great reward. Anansi returned to the spider and warned it of the god's wrath, telling the spider to go and hide in hopes that Chiuta would never get the chance to ask the spider any questions that might reveal the truth of the ram's death.

Meanwhile the god Chiuta told his wife what happened. The wife laughed and said, "Have you lost your mind husband? How on earth could a little spider make a thread strong enough to hold a ram? How in the world could that little spider hoist the ram up in a tree? Can't you see Anansi killed your ram and has blamed the poor spider?"

Chiuta was angry that he had been deceived and told his priests to fetch Anansi immediately. When the god's men came for him, Anansi assumed that they would carry him up to the palace in the sky for his reward. So Anansi went along willingly, striding into the great throne room as if he owned the place. "Well, what is my reward for finding the killer of your ram?" he proudly asked Chiuta.

This enraged Chiuta so much that he kicked Anansi, splitting him into many pieces. Chiuta's power surged over Anansi as he struggled in pain upon the ground and he changed. Anansi was no longer a man, but a spider with long legs. "There, now you have become that which you tried to betray! You will be my servant now. I will take your lands and you will hear the prayers of the people. And you will spend your days helping them! That will be your burden now!" Then Chiuta laughed and sent Anansi back to the Earth below.

Back on Earth, Anansi was compelled to hear the prayers and aid those who called upon Chiuta. He had no choice, for the power of Chiuta's curse was strong. Hideous and enslaved, Anansi was sad for a long time, but as the years passed, he learned how to gain joy from helping those who deserved aid and tricking those who did not. He lived the rest of his days as a man who looked like and was indeed a spider.

After many years of service, he was called back up to the sky palace to live with the other gods and was not seen on Earth again. The people were sad, for they had gotten used to his appearance and his help. But the stories of Anansi lived on in the people's hearts for all time.

The End of Innocence

By Anita Martinez

A tale of young Es-huh, the trusted slave of Namtar the servant god of Lamasthu. As an adult, Es-huh crosses the path of Aavi in the first novel. This story takes place in the realm of Babylonia.

The little girl skipped past the well-guarded doors of the large house and into the busy kitchen, carrying a small jug of water from the well in the court-yard. As soon as the steamy warmth of the large room touched her skin she slowed; whatever happened she must not spill the water or get in the way of any of the cook-slaves, or she would surely be punished. She walked carefully, quietly, to a heavy wooden table, avoiding harried-looking, flour-covered scullery maids and placed the jug next to the others that were already being used to fill the soup pot.

Having finished her job, she looked about for Cook, intending to ask if there was anything else she could do. She found the bustle and activity of the kitchen far more interesting than the work that she would be put to when Mother found her.

Not seeing Cook anywhere, the girl walked out into the courtyard and sat down on a bench by the well. She reclined, glorying in the feel of the sunshine on her skin and the light breeze that lifted tendrils of her hair to wave gaily at the clouds. She knew that Mother would be furious.

Looking around, the girl surveyed the courtyard. At the far end, the gate used by visitors and by the supply wagons that brought those items necessary to maintain the luxurious lifestyle of the house stood open. Ahh… another wagon would be coming soon, then. The girl decided to get a little closer and watch; maybe it would bring something interesting.

As she moved toward the gate she peered back over her shoulder and scanned the surrounding walls to make sure she was not being followed. Deciding that she was too exposed, she moved to the side wall of the yard where there was a thin line of shade. She instantly regretted her choice. Her nose filled with a stench that nearly gagged her. She ran, hoping to get past the odor. She came to a door that she had never seen unlocked before, and curiosity got the better of her.

The girl slowed and peeked through the crack in the door, trying to locate the source of the odor. She did not expect to see horses. She had heard the stable lads boast about the magnificence of the stalls and the rich grains and hay and cool water that the animals received. She had never actually seen a pig, but she had heard people say that someone stank like a pig, so maybe that was what was inside.

She had to pry the door open a bit more before she could see inside. There were pens made of metal bars that went from floor to ceiling along both sides of the hall, for it was, in essence, a hall. The actual pens were about the size of a small bedroom. Some were empty, but several were occupied... by people!

But, oh! These people, men and women (though not in the same pens with each other) alike, were thin and dirty. Many wore clothes that hung in tatters and did little to cover them. A few had sores on their bodies and most were missing teeth. They stood or sat listlessly on the fetid straw that covered the stone floors. Each pen had a wooden bucket that could hold about as much water as the jug she had carried earlier. In the corners of the pens were brown piles that attracted clouds of buzzing flies.

Terrified, the girl turned to run, but a hand closed around her arm.

"Stop right there, girl! What do you think you're doing here? This is no place for such as you!"

Fearfully, the girl looked up at her captor. He was not old. He had the beginning of a beard, and hair that reached to his shoulders. He was well-muscled, and the grip on her arm attested to his strength. He wore a training harness, a kilt, sandals and little else. His skin was brown, and shiny with the sweat of recent exertion. He did not exactly look scary... but the girl was frightened nonetheless.

"Who are you? Wha-what is this horrible place? How do you know who I am?" The questions tumbled out as nervous whimpers.

The young man looked down on her, a stern look on his face.

"I am Oloth. I am in training for the House Guard." This he said rather imperiously, as if it made him someone important. "It is evident by your clothes that you are a house slave. The scum in there are no more than worker slaves for the fields and mines. You soil yourself by being so near to them. What are you doing out here, anyway?"

The girl looked down at her feet. "I'm Es-huh," she mumbled. "I just wanted to get out of the house and see something interesting. It's so boring in there! There's so much more happening in the kitchen and out in the courtyard..."

"Do you have any idea how much trouble you could get into? Where do you belong? I will take you right back before anything can happen to you."

"Why should it make a difference? Nothing happens to you out here.. Nothing happens to the kitchen slaves…" Her voice trailed off as Oloth pulled her back across the courtyard toward the entrance to the kitchen.

Mother was madder than Es-huh had ever seen her. She met Oloth and Es-huh at the top of the kitchen stairs and immediately grabbed her by her other arm. She thanked Oloth tersely and, without another word, marched the girl up to their quarters. The maids they passed turned away, wide-eyed, having never seen Mother in such a fury.

In the sleeping room, Mother practically threw Es-huh down into a corner. "What - do - you - think - you - were - doing?" she hissed through clenched teeth.

Es-huh began to sob quietly. "I just wanted to do something interesting," she whispered. "Outside is so nice! I was only in the courtyard… what could happen there? They won't put me in one of those pens, will they?"

Mother's face softened for just a moment, then hardened again.

"Ahh… you saw the pens. Child, it is time we had a talk. I had hoped to wait a little longer, but I see you have a strength of spirit that will get you into more trouble than you can possibly imagine if you don't understand the way of things in our world. You have grown up hearing the word 'slave'. Do you know what that really means, my daughter?" she asked.

"The kitchen slaves work in the kitchen and help Cook," replied Es-huh, "… and Oloth said that those dirty people in the pens were worker slaves, but they looked awful. I wouldn't want to eat anything that one of them had touched!" she grimaced.

"Es-huh, a slave is somebody who belongs to someone else, just like a house or a wagon does. A slave must do whatever the master wants. Many are put to work, some are sold for profits, some are used in 'entertainments' for the master and some, if they have special skills or qualities, are chosen to fill more elevated positions in a household.

"Daughter… I am a slave. You are a slave. We are the property of the master of this house. I have the fortune to have some beauty and therefore was trained since I was your age to be a special servant to some master. Without those qualities, though, I might have been used as a scullery maid, someone to tend chickens or even worse! And there are much, much worse uses that female slaves can be put to."

Es-huh saw her mother shudder slightly. She answered, "I never want to be in a pen like an animal, Mother," too young to understand the reason for the shudder.

"You are better than that, my daughter. You will grow into beauty, and can aspire to the highest of positions. But you must protect your body. You must not let your skin turn brown and dry in the sun or your feet and hands become calloused like those of a common field slave. You must learn to serve your master respectfully and demurely. You must learn the rituals of service, prayer and praise."

Es-huh was silent, considering her mother's words. She remembered the squalor of the slave pens in the stinking hall with disgust and horror. She did not want to end up like that! She knew that she would do whatever she had to do to be a special servant like her mother was.

Her mother continued, "In this house we all serve the goddess Lamasthu. If you are to earn a good place in the service of our goddess, it is time to begin your training. You are young, but I believe you are old enough to understand the importance of the things that will be asked of you. Do you agree?"

Es-huh answered formally. "Yes, Mother. I wish to begin the training to become a high slave in service to Lamasthu. I will protect myself from anything that could make me unfit for that service. I will work hard and obey from now on."

Mother looked down at her daughter, a mixture of pride and sorrow in her eyes. She would miss her daughter when the messenger from the Namtar came that afternoon to take Es-huh to her new home in the City of the Gods.

Aavi and the Goddess Koshartu

By M. Scott Verne

Koshartu is a Canaanite goddess, the wife of the god Koshar U Khasis, whose name means "Skillful and Clever." Her name would then be a feminine version of Koshar, making it "The Skillful Goddess." There is not much known about Koshartu beyond the bare fact that she is Koshar U Khasis's wife. Koshar U Khasis is the Canaanite craftsman of the gods, who makes magical weapons, builds palaces, creates furniture, and is credited with being the first poet. This scene takes place during the time that Aavi is being held as a slave by the god Namtar, and gives a little more background as to how and why the gods buy slaves. It also gives a hint as to the reason that the gods left Earth.

"She's in here, Koshartu," said Namtar, the High Sulgi of Lamasthu's slaver temple. His muscular human body was incongruously completed by a hawk's head and brown and white striped wings. His sturdy legs revealed clawed bird talons in place of feet, though he had the hands of a normal human. Clothed in an umbra-colored toga that wrapped around his torso like a cloak caught in the wind, he held the door open as Koshartu entered his office.

The tall woman wore a long dress made from linen dyed deep purple. Two swathes of the fabric extended out from her shoulders and attached to gold bracelets on each arm.

She wore a golden headdress festooned with small bells that chimed as she walked. She carried a long elegant staff carved from a giraffe bone.

"You piqued my curiosity," Koshartu said. "Now I have to see your Princess."

"Looks like she is still asleep," Namtar noted as

they entered the room. Koshartu approached Aavi's cage.

"Where did you find her? Is she really of royal blood?"

"Well, as you are one of my best clients . . . she's not as far as I know. I picked the name 'Princess' because she's as unblemished as one. The girl was found by one of my scouts in the Asian realm, unbonded, alone, and wandering in the woods."

"The Asian Realm? She's not originally from there, that much is certain," Koshartu chuckled, looking more intently at the girl in the cage. "I would say your princess might be an enchanted woman. The Greek and Celtic gods are always enchanting someone, especially pretty young girls. With that flaxen-colored hair, more likely she's Celtic. But how did she end up unbonded? Could she have been banished? You would think they'd want to keep her after making her permanently clean and removing her navel. I still don't know why they bothered with that. It could be part of a curse, I suppose. Perhaps it means she cannot bear children."

Namtar listened patiently as the goddess voiced all her opinions. "That makes sense Koshartu. I hadn't considered she might be barren. If she is cursed in some other way, she shows no sign of it," he replied, slowly nodding his head.

Aavi, roused by their voices, slowly opened her eyes. She had cried herself to sleep after witnessing the whipping of another slave in her stead. Although Aavi had not been touched, she had felt the pain of the lash as much as the poor girl who had taken her place. Physical and emotional pain still swirled through her body. Too overwrought to react to the visitors, she merely watched as the High Sulgi and a woman dressed in purple stared at her through the cage bars. Aavi noticed the woman was slightly taller than the High Sulgi. She had dark hair and dark eyes that were outlined to make them look more distinct.

"You did say she has lost her memory," the woman was saying. "Perhaps that's part of the curse too."

"Logical as always, Koshartu. Ah, she awakens. Notice her eyes."

Aavi then sat up, her gaze switching back and forth between the two. She wasn't sure if she was allowed to speak, so remained silent, waiting to see what would happen next.

Koshartu leaned in for a closer look and stared at Aavi. "Yes. They're an unusual color. Almost violet. Can she talk?"

Namtar crossed his arms and looked sternly at Aavi. "Princess, say greetings to Koshartu the goddess. I've brought her up here just to see you"

"H-hello, Goddess Ko..shar..tu," Aavi responded hesitantly, hoping she had said the name correctly.

"A very melodic and soothing voice, despite her slowness. I'd wager she could sing quite nicely if given the proper training. Have you ever sung before, Princess?" asked Koshartu.

Aavi thought about that question. For a second, she seemed to recall having sung and having enjoyed it, but there was no memory she could connect to the feeling. "I know what singing is, but I don't remember ever doing so. I-I'm sorry."

Namtar interjected. "She's like this with everything, Koshartu. She seems to have no memories of anything. She doesn't even know how to dress herself. If you do buy her, keep that in mind. I don't want you bringing her back for a refund due to her lack of such common knowledge. Mind you, Princess is very teachable. She's had many training breakthroughs since I've taken her in hand." He gave Aavi a stern look, a smug smile curled up at the corners of his yellow beak.

"Does she really repel dirt? I'd like to see that."

Namtar walked towards his large desk. Just beyond it in the corner of the room was a palm tree in a large clay urn. He picked up a big handful of wet earth, and then walked back. "Watch this." He threw the wet dirt directly at Aavi. Aavi shrieked, flinched, and tried to cover her face as she felt the mud spatter all over her body. "Now stand up, Princess, and come over here," Namtar commanded.

"Y-yes High Sulgi." Reluctantly, Aavi complied. She stood up, her naked white skin now marred by a thousand dark speckles of dripping mud and wet debris. As she turned and took just a few steps towards Namtar and Koshartu, the wet dirt simply fell away or disappeared. Aavi stood inches away from the two deities, the bars of her cage the only thing between them.

Namtar smiled as he pointed at Aavi. "You see? The dirt refuses to stay upon her. It's a very interesting effect, don't you think?"

"Yes, it's fascinating to watch, though I'd hoped she might glow or burst into flame to get rid of the dirt. I see the lack of her navel too. Very subtle. You almost don't notice at first," Koshartu's running commentary continued. "I can always use a new addition to my slave menagerie. The more unusual the better. You know, I still get comments about that centaur you sold me last season. Maybe I could put this one in the middle of a room and my guests could throw filth at her and watch it fall right off," Koshartu laughed.

Aavi didn't like the idea of anything being thrown at her. She was certain it would hurt and winced just thinking about it. Her hands drifted over to hide her missing navel as they spoke about it and laughed at her. She felt humiliated, but there was nothing she could do, or others might suffer for her disobedience.

Koshartu looked Aavi in the eye. "So, you have no idea where you're from?"

Aavi looked furtively at Namtar then back to Koshartu. "No, I really don't. I don't remember who I am or this . . . City of the Gods we are in. None of this is familiar to me."

"You are an interesting riddle," Koshartu began, but the words dried up as she suddenly felt a mild discomfort as she stared at Aavi. However, whatever had given her pause was not enough to sour her interest. "I'll be here to bid on her Namtar. I'd love to discover what other mysteries she might hold. Thank you for an interesting demonstration."

"Of course, it was my pleasure." Namtar gestured toward the door.

Aavi despaired as they casually walked away from her. She held onto the bars of the cage and lowered her head, watching her tears splatter on the floor.

As the two gods reached the door, Koshartu turned and looked back at Aavi, a trace of recognition passing over her face. "You know, there's something about your Princess that makes me think I may have seen her at some point back on Earth. Maybe just before we were exiled."

"Exiled?" Feathers on Namtar's brow fluttered as he turned to look at Koshartu.

She broke her gaze, turning towards Namtar. "Well, that's what I call it. Perhaps you Babylonian deities were more willing to leave than we Canaanites. Your days had passed, but we still had many worshippers on Earth."

"Your Pantheon never had as many followers as ours, you know that," Namtar responded pridefully.

"Yes, yes, but we still had followers when the great leaving came. That was my point."

Namtar nodded his head in the affirmative. "I see. I meant no insult Koshartu, please accept my apology."

There were a few seconds of tense silence as they left Namtar's office and walked along the hall to the stairs. Koshartu turned to face the slaver god, finally replying. "None taken. Now, when is Princess going to be on the auction block?

"Tomorrow, around noon."

"Very well, but I'm not going to pay as much for her as I did for that centaur."

Namtar's beak showed the hint of a smile. "I don't know what she'll go for, you know how these auctions are."

"That's half the fun, Namtar."

"May the blessings of Lamasthu shine upon you, Koshartu."

Koshartu walked down the stairs and into the slave sellers' den towards the exit as Namtar watched her go. He leaned on the railing, his sharp yellow beak curled up in a smile. "Tomorrow is going to be a good day. A very good day," he thought. Then Namtar called out to his servant, "Es-huh, bring some food and drink up here for our Princess!"

Es-huh answered her master from the bottom of the stairs, "Yes High Sulgi. I'll get the meal now..."

Every Road Has Its Toll

By Wynn Mercere

This adventure of D'Molay and Sergius takes place several years before the events of City of the Gods: Forgotten

D'Molay found trips to the Celtic lands pleasant. The roads were smooth, the villages were mostly free of troublesome gods, and the Celts kept their noses in their own business for the most part. Unless a visitor was mindlessly brutal or brutally stupid, plenty of profit or pleasure could be found in the company of the lords and lackeys of this realm. So, when the High Priest of Zeus asked D'Molay to extract a calf from the livestock auction in New Camelot, he didn't hesitate to take on the job. It was a simple, straightforward mission to buy an animal, even if that calf was in truth a bastard son of Zeus transformed and hidden in a herd to cover

evidence of his infidelity. Zeus' wife Hera had not discovered his transgression, but the plan was still on the verge of failure. Zeus, immortal and distant, had forgotten that death still roamed the City and its realms. The farmer to whom he had entrusted his son had been killed by a wyrm. Today, his herds were being sold to pay for funeral rites and a tomb.

Retrieving the boy from the sale would pay D'Molay very, very well. So well, in fact, that he had invited his old friend and occasional tracking partner Sergius to come along. D'Molay had little use for money beyond his basic needs, but Sergius bore the curse of Roman ambition. He was always talking up some new enterprise that he hoped would provide a living easier than slaving or running errands for the gods. Lately he'd been dreaming about opening a tavern. D'Molay counted it just another of his ill-conceived notions, but listened patiently to Sergius's speculations on how much he would have to charge for wine and food, how many serving wenches to employ, and what part of the City was the thirstiest. His friend's conversation dried up, however, as they drew near New Camelot and had to concentrate on threading their way through other travelers, at times riding separately as each found his own path around obstacles.

The road was choked with farmers driving animals in for the sale and merchant wagons loaded with feed and tack to peddle to those who would purchase them. Milling between the herds were individuals of all ages and descriptions heading into town for the auction. Progress was annoyingly slow. D'Molay had to rein in his horse several times to avoid trampling careless children. Enough was enough when he noticed that Sergius was riding with feet spread wide purely for the fun of nudging the oblivious in the back of the head with his hobnailed boots.

"Zeus' son will be sold, skinned, and tanned at this rate," D'Molay said, reaching over to tap Sergius on the arm. "The woods will be faster." He guided his horse off the road and into the trees with Sergius following closely. Fifty paces in they found a narrow deer track that paralleled the road. The trees around it towered and the way was dark, but mounds of interesting bright flowers grew in clumps along the trail. D'Molay committed them to memory so that he could illustrate the trail accurately on the map he'd been working on. With nothing to block their way, they soon passed the traffic on the road and emerged from the trees. A short canter across a sparse stretch of pasture delivered them to the lot just outside town where the crowds were gathering.

"Look at this confusion," Sergius said as they dismounted to tie their horses to a stone road marker. "Why aren't these farmers in a queue? I could run a more organized auction dead drunk on Etruscan wine."

D'Molay patted his mare's neck to settle her. "Just push past. Most of these people aren't here to buy. They're just -- "

"In our way," Sergius smirked. He picked a short club out of his saddlebag and flipped it cockily into the air. It spun twice before coming to rest with a slap in his palm. "Don't worry, D'Molay. I actually do like people, as long as they're making me money. I won't break too many heads."

"I can ask for nothing more," D'Molay responded, unconsciously assuming his old manners of a sarcastic French courtier as he wondered why his force-fond partner had ever left the joys of the Roman army. Nonetheless, his hand drifted to his hip to check the readiness of his own weapon as they moved into the mass of Celts and approached the auction platform. D'Molay was aware of some additional grumbling from Sergius, but his words were lost in a din of booing that suddenly went up from the crowd. Their ire seemed directed at a short man on the platform who was rapidly losing control of the event. In response to the booing, he had scurried to the edge of the stage and flapped his arms for silence. This only encouraged the hecklers in the crowd to mock him with quacking noises.

"Get on with it!" a dark man near D'Molay shouted at the platform. "Ain't got all day!"

"What's the hold up?" D'Molay asked him.

"Dunno," the man shrugged. "Stupid fool won't start the sale." He began to shout again, clearly enjoying the opportunity to bellow.

Sergius leaned in close to D'Molay's ear. "I see we haven't missed anything."

D'Molay nodded then gestured toward the animal pens beyond the platform before turning his back and heading that way. He knew his partner was following from the indignant yelps and curses of people the impatient Roman was shoving out of his way. When he reached the pens, D'Molay was faced with a lumpish herdsman guarding the livestock to be sold. The man's face was framed with dark curly hair that hadn't seen even an accidental washing in months. One of his fat thumbs was carefully guiding a small knife with a chipped blade under the rind of a bluish-white cheese as he leaned against a pole inset with iron rings. Two skinny goats tied together to one of the metal hoops nattered loudly, hopeful a scrap would fall from the herdsman's knife.

"Now that's a stink worthy of note," Sergius said of the herdsman, his lunch, and the smell of goats as he caught up with D'Molay. He swiped his wristband across the underside of his nose to appease his senses with the comforting smell of oiled leather. "Hurry it up, D'Molay, before we're permanently mired in manure."

"I can see why you never took a soldier's retirement as a farmer," D'Molay said.

"I'm no fool," Sergius shot back, opening his arms wide to encompass the mire of mud, straw and animal waste that surrounded them. "I chose glamorous adventure."

The two old friends shared a laugh while the herdsman barely glanced at them. D'Molay visually searched the huddle of calves in the back section of the pen. The son of Zeus was easy to pick out when one knew what to look for. One of the russet brown calves was marked by a telltale golden spot on its right ear, the thumbprint of his immortal father. All that need be done now was to prevent the calf from going to auction. For that purpose D'Molay had prepared a bluff.

"I have a contract of sale," he lied to the herdsman as he eased the end of his rolled-up map of the realms an inch out of his coat. "Point me to your master so I can pay."

The man levered a fresh glob of cheese into his maw and sucked on it slowly as he stared at the butt of parchment. At the sound of a grunt, D'Molay instinctively thrust his arm out sideways to prevent Sergius from moving forward to pick up and pitch the slow-mannered herdsman in with the swine. "Patience, Sergius."

The herdsman blinked at them doubtfully as he swallowed his food. "Sir Cedric mayn't be takin' money this late," he mumbled.

"A Celt who won't take coin. That's new," Sergius said. There was a low threat in his voice.

"He'll take mine," D'Molay smoothed over. "Is he inside?" The herdsman betrayed his boss with an uncertain glance toward a door of the attached building framed by an arch of stone. "Good."

Leaving the indecisive herdsman and his foul smells in their wake, Sergius and D'Molay entered the building and stopped to look into the first room they found. In it, a red-haired man garbed in the style of a village leader or minor noble sat at a table before a counting box. He started at the sight of them, as if he'd been caught napping. His fingers quickly scrabbled across the table to grab a stick of charcoal lying atop a parchment list.

"Enter, enter," he said, waving them in. He then pointed at an hourglass that had almost run through its sand. "If you're here to buy, be quick. There will be no direct sales once the auction starts."

D'Molay immediately displayed his money pouch and the man nodded in approval.

"There is a calf outside with a blazoned ear," D'Molay said. "That's the one we're buying."

"Calves bring ten, with a presale premium of five," the Celt said flatly, extending his hand.

D'Molay fished out fifteen gold coins and exchanged them for a long strip of rope attached to a strap with a leather tag threaded onto it. A symbol was burned onto the tag.

"This shows I've paid?"

"It does. Collar the calf and my man will let you take it off the lot." D'Molay handed the lead to Sergius who left to secure the animal. The money counter looked up expectantly. "Is there something else you want to buy?"

D'Molay was doubtful about the next part of his mission, but his job was merely to make the delivery, not see it through to its end. He placed a hundred more gold coins from Zeus on the table. "I would like this money to be added to the final auction tally due the estate of the man whose calf I just bought. An anonymous friend wants to help his family."

The man's eyes lit up. D'Molay immediately suspected that the bounty would go no further than the greedy fellow's own pockets. Woe be to him if he indeed stole the coins, but that wouldn't be D'Molay's problem. Zeus would see him punished. Setting snares for humans was always a game of the gods.

When D'Molay stepped back out into the sunlight, Sergius was waiting with the calf in tow. "Change him back into a boy," Sergius said quietly. "He can ride with one of us easily and we can travel faster."

D'Molay reached for the cord he wore around his neck and worked the enchanted amulet Zeus' priest had given him for just that purpose free from the collar of his coat. "Agreed. But let's do it back in the woods where no one from the auction will see and think we've cheated them somehow."

The sounds of bidding and the lowing of livestock faded behind them as they collected their horses and headed back to the woodland trail. They rode into the cover of the trees, the calf drawn along by the rope Sergius held. Halfway down the deer path, where the bright flowers grew, D'Molay dismounted. Sergius followed suit and walked over to the calf, slackening the rope. The playful young bull danced a few steps away, its hooves crushing a clump of bright amber petals.

"Trespass!"

D'Molay and Sergius came to full alert at the sound of the scratchy, bitter voice.

"Who's there?" D'Molay demanded to know. He and Sergius both peered into the woods for the source of the complaint.

"Trespass!"

The single word came again, this time in a chorus of voices, some as rough as the first and others pure and melodic.

"I'm mounting up," Sergius said, pulling the rope back toward his horse.

The calf suddenly froze and squealed in pain. D'Molay looked over to see one of its rear legs being stretched back from its body. A cluster of small beings, some delicate and winged, others covered with thick, knobbed skin, had seized the calf's hoof. A crushed flower dangled from some mud stuck to its underside. Tiny hands and claws tore at the calf's fetlock.

"Faeries!" D'Molay yelled, a warning which was immediately followed by a third denunciation of trespass delivered in a single, sad, whisper. As the word's last breathy syllable faded, a thick mist rose up to blind and deafen them. D'Molay could just barely hear Sergius cursing somewhere nearby. Reaching out sightlessly, he grabbed randomly in hopes of securing Zeus' son, but dozens of small hands pushed his arms in the wrong direction. Then a hundred more pressing palms yanked his feet out from under him. D'Molay fell, sliding down a shaft that had opened in the earth. He rolled a half dozen times before he managed to stop and right himself. He immediately called for Sergius, but there was no answer. His mind was working out whether this bode good or ill when a flash of light dispelled the mist.

"Sir Geas escaped," a sultry female voice announced as D'Molay's eyes adjusted to the brightness and the startling proximity of a curvaceous body. "But you didn't, so you must be the one to pay."

"Pay . . . for what?"

D'Molay knew he was at peril of falling into the enchanting spell of the beautiful creature. He hardened his heart and narrowed his eyes, focusing on the devilishly pointed tips of her ears to avoid the deep loveliness of her green eyes and full pink lips. She took a step back from him as if she knew of his determination to keep his wits.

"Your calf destroyed our blossoms. Do you know how long it takes to grow firedrops? Children of our children will be born and die before new seeds can stretch their way into new blooms."

"I'm sorry," D'Molay said cautiously, watching the female pace slowly about the chamber. He could now see he was in a cell. Bars crisscrossed an opening above his head. "But what could I possibly pay that is of equal value?"

The faerie glanced briefly toward the overhead bars as a muffled, repeating scraping noise reached the cell. D'Molay kept his eyes pinned to his captor, even as his hopes rose to meet the sound. He'd bet the remaining gold in his pouch that it was Sergius trying to dig him out.

"I am a Faerie Nymph. Your people say we like sweets and babies and the finest spun silk. You've none of those, have you?"

43

D'Molay shook his head in the negative, wondering if striking her would do more harm than good. He could be certain of nothing where faeries were involved. What he'd heard of their sorcery was enough to chill his blood. He silently urged Sergius to dig faster.

"Well, it wouldn't matter if you did," she scoffed. "What they say of us are lies."

"Then you'll have to tell me what you want," D'Molay ventured, "if everything I think I know is wrong."

She folded her arms and regarded him with a smug expression. "Since

you are willing to admit you know nothing, I will teach you something." In an instant, she closed the distance between them and D'Molay felt her lips press against his and her fingers play about his throat. Before he realized what she was doing, she had snatched the magic amulet from his neck.

She pulled away from him triumphantly. "What we really like is magic. This trinket of yours has saved your life."

"You don't want to take that," D'Molay tried to bargain. "It belongs to Zeus, the main god of the Olympian Realm."

The Faerie Nymph began to laugh, barely managing to get her words out between giggles. "That bearded old man who sits on his mountain? We're not afraid of him," she said. Then as quickly as her demeanor had turned jolly, it flipped to mock sadness. "Oh, poor man. Will losing this get you in trouble?"

D'Molay knew her sympathy was false but wanted to keep her talking to buy time. Perhaps Sergius would break through, or he would have a chance to steal the amulet back. "Not really, but it will be bad for the calf."

The faerie had the reaction D'Molay had hoped for. She seemed curious about what the necklace had to do with the calf. "How so?"

"It will never regain its true form without the charm. It will live and die as a cow."

D'Molay let the silence spread between them and told her nothing more.

"And what was 'it' before 'it' became a destroyer of firedrops?" she eventually asked.

"Release me and we can find out together."

Her laughter resumed. "I think not! You've paid your bill and I'm not in the market for any tricks." She spoke several strange words and mist again filled the room, cloaking her form. The last thing to disappear in the fog was the Faerie's face, her lips curved in a mocking smile. Then D'Molay was seized again, a multitude of tiny hands lifting and maneuvering him through the cloudy dark until he was dropped painfully to the ground. He pushed himself quickly into a sitting position, guessing from the feel of trodden dirt beneath his palms that he was back on the road. The mist began to disappear.

"Sergius! Over here!"

His friend rushed toward him, extending a hand to help him stand. "So I dug like a dog for nothing. How'd you get away?"

"I had to give up the amulet," D'Molay confessed.

"You mean we'll have to take him back to Olympus as a calf? . . . Damn. The trip back is going to take forever. At least I'm sure Zeus can change him back.once we get there," Sergius replied

"I'll assume that means you haven't lost the calf... I mean the boy."

"He's fine." Sergius lifted the haft of his dirty shovel to rest against his shoulder and pointed off to the left with his free hand. "He's over there, chewing on some flowers."

D'Molay turned as pale as the mist. "Let's get him and go - and just hope those flowers don't belong to the faeries too!"

For the Right Price

By Wynn Mercere

Residents of the City of the Gods see more wonders than men of old Earth ever imagined. Living among the gods, boys like Nianzu and Parham can see that many of the old stories told by mortals about deities are completely true. However, doubt can intrude to rest heavily in striving adolescent hearts.

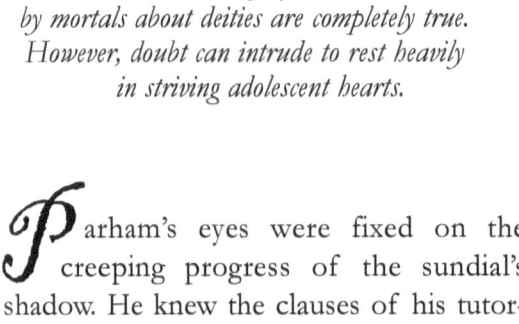

*P*arham's eyes were fixed on the creeping progress of the sundial's shadow. He knew the clauses of his tutoring contract by heart; if the teacher did not appear by the appointed time, his day would be his own. For a youth of only fourteen years in the City of the Gods, such freedom was a rare thing.

"Almost," he said, palms already pressing into the wild grasses that covered the ground outside The Good Village *(a training center in the City of the Gods)*, ready to lever him up from his seat in the mid-morning sun. Calmly waiting next to him, the boy called Nianzu was not watching the clock. Instead, he was carefully sketching the tangled blades of the plants around them upon a scrap of parchment and making notes in his own language, which Parham could not read.

"Why are you in such a hurry to leave?" Nianzu asked. "Yesterday you told teacher you couldn't wait to discuss the story of the ocean of milk."

Parham unconsciously moved his right hand from the grass to grip the upper folds of his robe, the traditional position among his people for debating an important point. Fist of power resting on heart of honor, he explained his apparent change of mind. "That's because I have evidence to present that proves it didn't happen the way she said." Parham ignored the smirk this statement created on Nianzu's face. The eastern boy might think him pompous, but every opportunity to give a speech was important practice for Parham's coveted role as a Civil Priest, the elite legal class of the City.

"We're supposed to draw greater truths from stories, not pick at them. Besides, what do you know about it? Unless Shiva himself set you upon his knee and told you otherwise."

Parham couldn't help but scowl at Nianzu, who immediately broke out into a broad grin as he achieved his goal of annoying him. He was beginning to suspect that Nianzu learned as much from teasing and manipulating his classmates as he did from his scrolls. But as far as the aspiring lawyer was concerned, Nianzu's tolerance for the vagaries of myth was unacceptable. There was truth, and there were fantasies excused as 'greater truth.' Suddenly Parham's irritation vanished as he realized that concept was a promising subject for a future speech. He got to his feet, pacing with renewed interest as lines of argument fought for prominence in his mind.

A few minutes later he was distracted by the noise of several other students scrambling from their positions on the lawn and running off. The teacher's time to come had passed, and all were free. Nianzu put away his art tools, looking up at him.

"Shall we try again today?"

Parham nodded as Nianzu too stood up. "What's next on the list?"

"Beads. Green ones."

The two boys walked away from The Good Village toward the market stalls of the Temple District. Along the walls of the Great Hindu Temple, carts of all sizes, and blankets flung across the ground, were filled with wares. The aromas of foods, perfumes, spices and animals mingled into a cloud of sensory confusion. Fortunately, Parham and Nianzu knew the market well, and made straight for a small tent behind a curry cart. Its flap stood open in welcome as the boys sidled past a large Afrik woman who was examining necklaces hanging from a line pegged outside. The proprietor, a short, dark man with heavy locks of styled hair, raised a bushy eyebrow at the unexpected sight of teenage boys in his shop.

"Well now. What could you two possibly want here?" he asked, getting directly to the point.

While Nianzu placidly ignored the brusque hint and began sifting through a basket of loose baubles, Parham looked the man in the eye, taking his time before giving an answer. The shopkeeper was one of his own realmsmen, so Parham immediately began to negotiate as his father had taught him.

"Where are your better beads?" Parham asked. "I'm not interested in the cheap ones you leave out for anyone to pocket."

The man opened his mouth to protest the boy's disrespect toward his wares; then he noticed Nianzu's hands in a basket. "You! Bring those fingers of yours over here. And you," he said skeptically to Parham, "show me your purse."

Only one of the merchant's demands was met. Nianzu joined them, but Parham's money pouch remained safely hidden in his robes. Parham's disregard of the shopkeeper's demand was meant to showcase his confidence when dealing with adults, and he was sure it was the right move even though he sensed that Nianzu was uncomfortable with this slight to an elder. It compelled his friend to speak up and play the role of polite customer.

"We want to buy some small gem beads to offer to Tara," Nianzu said.

"Beads for Tara? Tara doesn't need beads."

The boys turned to face the heavy-set shopper whom they had seen outside. The merchant responded to her interruption with a muted groan.

"Not today, Sauda," he said, waving his arms at the Afrik woman as if she were a goose he could shoo away. "Go convince someone else you know all the gods' secrets. I'm just here to sell these damn beads."

"The secret chamber of the goddess Tara requires the right offering to enter," Parham declared, boldly implying he was privy to some of the City's secrets himself. "Why not beads?"

"We've tried other things," Nianzu volunteered. "Spices, oil, flowers, a rabbit." The woman laughed heartily at this, grabbing the edge of a table to keep from doubling over.

"Men - young or old, they choose the worst gifts for women!" she said.

Parham frowned. He hated being ridiculed. "Sell me ten of those beads," he said abruptly, pointing at ones heaped in a hanging pot above the shopkeeper's head. Rattled by the woman's laughter, he forgot to haggle, and paid more that he should. The shopkeeper flashed a victorious smile as he pocketed Parham's coins.

"I'm sorry I tried to throw you out, Sauda," he said. "If you can make all my customers buy so quickly, and at such fair prices, you are welcome to visit me every day."

Parham shoved the beads into his pouch and slunk out of the store. Nianzu lingered, intrigued by the lively woman and what she might know. He had already noticed many interesting things about her. There were more charms, pins, inscribed ribbons and tiny effigies attached to her garments than fashion called for. Only a few of them were from her Afrik culture. Nianzu recognized the others by their shapes. Greek, Hindu, Mayan and Egyptian trinkets were scattered among strips of fabric imprinted with the writing of the Celts and Babylonians. There were even Nordic bone runes on the buckles of her shoes.

"Am I ugly, boy?" she asked as Nianzu stared at her feet. "Why don't you look at my face? It's very pretty."

Nianzu felt his face flush a bit as he looked up. "I - "

"Nianzu!" Parham called from outside. "Let's go!"

He bowed to a smirking Sauda and gratefully seized upon his friend's impatience as an excuse to leave.

Nianzu had to hurry after Parham, who was already striding with determined purpose toward the nearest entrance to the Great Hindu Temple. The huge structure housed the altars of many gods. Unlike other sacred places in the City, access was not restricted by priests or guards. Anyone could come inside at any hour and wander the rooms at will. The valuables on display, golden idols and gem-encrusted relics, were protected from thieves by powerful magic. But another deterrent to mischief was the sheer convolution of the temple structure itself. There were halls within halls, upper and lower floors with secret compact levels hidden between them, and other architectural trickery. Chambers changed their locations, shifting like clouds in the sky. The complex was a vast house of illusion and misdirection, with one legendary chamber most hidden.

The boys had been trying to find Tara's sanctuary for many months. They had overheard a conversation between two Civil Priests about how important Tara was to all the rest of the gods. Parham had become obsessed with finding out why she was so important and hoped to find the answers in her sanctuary. On each visit to the huge Hindu Temple they tried a random path, having learned over time that any systematic exploration was futile due to the temple's magical space shifting. Today Parham chose a wide passage leading, it seemed, toward the center of the building, but its true destination was impossible to predict. When they came to an intersecting corridor lined with open archways, Nianzu chose an open room to their right. They continued to alternate choosing the next turn, moving at a steady pace through chambers dedicated to many gods and hallways adorned with exquisite artwork of legends and heroic deeds. It was Parham's turn to direct their steps when they came to a dead end. The boys stood before a stone wall carved with rows of raised lotus blossoms. The flowers had been painted in faint washes of color, giving each its own subtle hue. Parham exhaled a frustrated sigh and turned immediately to retrace their steps to the intersection. Then he noticed Nianzu was lingering, and waited. He watched his friend pace slowly along the length of the wall.

"Do you think pressing something would open a door?" Parham asked. Rumor held that hidden doorknobs and levers were sometimes disguised by ornate designs or hidden behind statuary. Not waiting for Nianzu's opinion, he stepped forward and began fiddling with the stems and petals on the wall. He succeeded only in staining his fingers with flecks of colorful paint.

"I was just counting them," Nianzu said as Parham tried to flick the paint dust from his hands. Parham glanced up to make his own tally, noting the three rows of seven lotuses.

"What for?"

"Chag tsal lha yi tsog nam gyal po, Lha dang mi am chi yi ten ma," Nianzu recited.

"What?" Parham asked. He was fluent only in his native language and Panthos, the new tongue which all now spoke. It was created by the Council and adopted as the official language of the City so that business could be easily conducted across all the realms. Parham classified Nianzu as a studious geek, but his boring interest in old languages sometimes came in handy

"It means, 'Homage to you on whom the kings of gods, the gods themselves and all spirits rely.' It's from the old prayer books of the Tibetans."

Parham scoffed as the wall stood unchanged, showing no indication that Nianzu's words had any power. "Might as well say 'iftah ya simsim.' Let's go back." But Nianzu remained planted where he was.

"Why would I say words from your realm when we stand before a tribute to the twenty-one incarnations of Tara?"

Parham was only mildly annoyed by Nianzu's smug grin. It was easy to cast

his prickly pride aside in the face of their discovery. It was the first time they had found anything in the temple that openly declared Tara's presence somewhere within. "I knew I would pick the right turn!" Parham practically crowed.

He redoubled his efforts to find some movable point on the wall. After poking and scratching all over it, he cupped his palms over two raised flowers and butted the top of his head against the stone. Eventually he looked back over his shoulder at Nianzu, who was shaking his head and grinning at the poor results of his technique.

"Why aren't you helping me?' Parham complained. Nianzu shrugged.

"Look at what you've done."

Confused, Parham turned back to the wall, stepping back to see that the lotus flowers were no longer there. When he tried to move the wall by brute force, the carvings upon it completely changed. As if to mock him, the wall was now inscribed with raised figures that told the very story he had planned to argue with his teacher that day.

He was face to face with a carving of Shiva. The god held the emptied cup of bitter venom, which the stories told he had drunk to save the world from a flood of destruction. Beneath him, his rivals fell away in awe at the new powers Shiva gained from his sacrifice. Parham's frown at the lost chance of entering Tara's sanctum furrowed his brow. He squinted at the stone pictures that echoed the myth he'd been assigned to study by their teacher - a myth whose underpinnings Parham definitely did not accept as factual. How could deities, sages and magnificent treasures appear just because of perseverance? Why would the Hindu gods downplay their supernatural powers and pretend that so many things in their formative story resulted from the mundane and arduous activity of stirring up milk, even if the milk was an entire ocean and its mixing spoons a mountain and a hundred-headed serpent? The other gods were not so modest. They were more than happy to prove that they could create great things by their thoughts alone. Parham had a gut feeling that there was more to the Hindu story than a desire to instill a hard work ethic into their people. There had to be something more, something hidden.

"I don't believe this!" he exclaimed in frustration.

"That's probably why the temple made it for you," Nianzu said.

Just then Parham's eyes drifted over another part of the relief, the scene of the Hindu gods battling challengers for possession of the Water of Life. There stood the sage in the tale who supposedly sprang from the churning; but there was no ocean of milk anywhere near him, not even a puddle or wetted feet. He was just one figure holding the cup away from a distressed crowd that was grabbing for his prize as covetously as the gods.

"I knew it!" Parham exclaimed in triumph. He pointed out his discovery to Nianzu. "No ocean of milk, no ages of toil. Just as I was going to argue!"

"Remind me. Was your entire speech based on saying that the Hindu gods are liars? I don't think there's any chance of pleasing teacher with that idea," Nianzu cautioned.

"But they must be! Why would this different account appear here in their own temple if not to show truth to the worthy?" Nianzu started laughing at Parham's bold assertion that he was suddenly enlightened, but this did not deter the determined boy. "I was seeking the goddess and she sent this sign."

"Only you can judge. But I don't think we're going to get any closer to the secret chamber today and I'm hungry. Let's find a way out."

Parham followed Nianzu, still consumed by the implications of the carvings they'd seen. He trailed after his friend with little attention to where their steps were leading. It wasn't until a voice accosted him that his attention came back to the world at large.

"Two coins, boy," the impatient vendor demanded, holding a stick of fried dough at him. He'd apparently queued up behind Nianzu at a snack cart without noticing where he stood. Luckily, he liked that type of food and opened his pouch to pay.

It was then he saw that all the green beads he had purchased as an offering had vanished. *We didn't find Tara, but she found us,* Parham realized.

Protector

By Ken St. Andre

*This D'Molay tale occurs
shortly before events in City of
the Gods: Forgotten.*

D'Molay's head lay upon his arm, his arm upon the stained wooden table. He snored gently, responsible for the only sound in the room. His weather-beaten hat rested half on his dark hair, half on the rough, splintered planks. The flame of a single flickering candle reflected fifteen times from the careful pyramid of brass flagons that the adventurer had constructed over the course of the evening. Instead of letting the barmaid take his empty cups away and refill them, he had insisted on building his own monument to inebriation, until it stood five levels high, and he had finally gone to sleep.

Sometime after midnight, but hours before dawn, the last customer had left the Jolly Rajah Tavern. Only D'Molay remained, and he was unconscious. The owner, a sinister-looking man named Sergius, told the staff to leave his friend D'Molay alone, to let him sleep. He looked like he needed it. Haggard, hungry, almost incoherent when he entered the tavern shortly after sunset, D'Molay had eaten and drunk and babbled about something lost in the Necropolis of Anubis. He drank and drank and drank, and might have drank himself to death except that his friend began watering his ale, a bit more with each cup, after his fifth flagon. D'Molay never noticed. He certainly never noticed when the jackal-headed assassin entered the deserted tavern.

The assassin moved slowly, cautiously, silently - just another shadow in a room full of shadows. He had to work his way behind the adventurer. The table protected the man's vitals all too well from the front. He carried in his hand a nine-inch obsidian dagger, all razor-sharp, brittle black, glassy stone.

Yellowed canine teeth protruded from the pointed muzzle of the Jackal as he lifted his arm for the killing stroke. He stood directly behind D'Molay with the dagger-wielding arm poised high for a strike right below the shoulder and into the heart from behind. "In the name of the Lord Anubis, Weigher of Souls, I take your life and your soul, Desecrater!" he growled softly.

Something white flickered through the air and struck the assassin in the center of his ebon forehead, right between his large black eyes. A rectangle of ivory blossomed in the Jackal's head, standing out from his forehead like a signpost. The thunk of ivory splitting through bone did not wake D'Molay, nor did the clatter of an obsidian dagger lost from nerveless fingers, hitting D'Molay's leather jacket and falling aside on to the wooden tabletop. The dog-man yipped once as it slumped backwards into the wall and slid down into a crouching position with knees on either side of his chin. D'Molay snored on.

The candle guttered out. All was Stygian darkness inside the common room of the tavern. The only sound was a quiet snoring from the slumped shape at the table. Or was it a purring noise instead?

The scream of a woman cut through D'Molay's troubled dreams. He had been running, running between the tombs and mausoleums of the City of the Dead, carrying the Orb of Ra. Howling pursued him. Demonic forms darted out at him from the shadows, but they slipped away when he tried to cut them with his enchanted knife. His face and his arm ached from some forgotten injury, and there was a hard bruise across his chest. His throat felt dry and scratchy; his head ached, an intense pain as if someone was scooping out his brains with a spoon. A woman screamed. He opened his eyes...

. . . and saw a pyramid of stacked brass flagons not more than six inches in front of his nose. Morning light poured into the room through an open door and a few small windows in the eastern wall. He sat up abruptly and the pain in his chest where it had been resting against the edge of the wooden table faded. His hat fell off completely, revealing a head of sweat-matted hair so brown it was almost black, most of it curled and knotted in what was practically a helmet of hair. The woman's scream caused a jagged surge of pain through his skull.

"Stop that screaming!" he snapped. "Haven't you ever seen a drunk before? I'm not that hideous, even if I haven't shaved for days." His innate sense of humor rose to the surface even in the middle of his disorientation.

She stopped screaming, but pointed a trembling finger behind him. "Ja-ja-j," she stammered.

D'Molay turned and saw the dead assassin. Instead of fear, a rictus of triumph and disgust briefly contorted his features. As he turned, his elbow bumped the obsidian blade lying on the tabletop and sent it sliding into the pyramid of brass flagons with just enough force to jostle the whole unstable structure. The cup on the top fell off first, and as it did, the whole edifice came crashing down with a strident clangor of metal on metal.

D'Molay ignored the clatter and lurched to his feet. "A jackal-head," he mumbled, "favored slave of Anubis. I wonder what the son of a bitch was doing here. They don't usually bother with this part of the City."

He looked around curiously, his naturally keen faculties coming back to him rapidly. He observed the black stone blade on the tabletop. He saw that the Jackal had been directly behind him. He recognized the functional, form-fitting black tunic and soft-soled boots, the belt of knives and needles of bone, the barely visible tattoos of the Anubis cult - all marks of the god-sanctioned assassins.

"That dog was here last night to kill me," he said, more to himself than to the middle-aged tavern drab who had awakened him.

He looked closer and saw the lozenge of ivory protruding from the canine's forehead. He reached out and tugged it from the Jackal's head, which took a fair bit of effort to do. It was well and truly embedded in the skull. He found himself holding a piece of ivory about the size of a bar of soap. The edges had been filed down to knife-like sharpness. The convex center swelled up to give the strange object some mass. Engraved on each side of the tablet was the profile head of a cat. "Mafdet," He muttered.

Even with its sharp edges the ivory tablet seemed like an unlikely instrument of murder. D'Molay lifted it in his gloved hand to press the surface against his aching head. He felt a faint tingle of force magic! Some of the pain in his head subsided.

He slipped the ivory tablet into a pocket in his leather jacket. When he put it there, he felt something smooth and round. The two objects clacked against each other.

"What is your name?" D'Molay asked his awakener. In times of stress, accentuate the normal, like names, and regain control - he had always found such behavior a good way for coping with extraordinary situations.

"Netrilla, Master," she said tentatively, looking at D'Molay now instead of the corpse. "What should I do?"

"You had better do your job and clean up this mess," he replied, waving his hand at the chaos of flagons on the table and the floor. "Oh, and call the City guard. They will take care of the body. I think it would be best if I'm not here when they arrive, however."

"But what will I tell them?"

"Tell them the truth. You came to work and you found this body. Do you know who I am?"

"No, Master."

"That's good, then. It will take the guard a while to track me down, and I have a feeling that I may need the time. Go on, do as I said."

As the maid moved hesitantly toward the door, D'Molay turned to the corpse and rapidly examined it. He found a sleek carrying pouch belted to one hip and took it, belting it around his own waist. Then he scooped up the obsidian dagger, grabbed his hat and thrust it down on his head. He decided to exit through the kitchen, so he stepped around the bar, pushed through a doorway, and strode past chopping tables and free-standing stoves toward the rear entrance. The morning janitor was just coming in.

"Hey, you can't . . ." the man started to object. D'Molay just nodded, smiled, and pushed past him and out the back door before the man could do anything.

D'Molay strode quickly down the alleyway, stepping around or over piles of refuse, and staying away from the street beggars huddled in various doorways. Once out of the alley, he made his way as quickly as he could to his own small room in The Settlement. He needed time to clean himself up, and time to think.

As he walked, he reached into his pocket and pulled out the round thing. It was fairly heavy, a metallic sphere about three inches in diameter. It had a nice warm color, being as it was solid gold. D'Molay somehow knew that it was the Orb of Ra. And as he walked further, the memory of how it had come into his possession returned to him. The traps in the Necropolis were infamous, but it wasn't until the Guardians appeared that he felt any fear. By that time, he had already found the Orb, and after that it was sheer head-long flight until he somehow escaped. Instinctively he crossed himself. Perhaps a higher power had been looking after him.

Two Lion-Men guarded the entrance to the modest pyramidal temple of Mafdet in the Egyptian quarter of the City of the Gods. One stood on each side of the gold-plated front doors. They did not carry weapons, other than a broad-bladed dagger at the belts of their hyena-furred tunics, but simply stood with arms folded over their massive chests, claws extended and gleaming. Their long tufted tails swayed behind them, almost in time together, and their broad black noses twitched with every new scent wafted to them on the early afternoon breeze. From time to time a cat-headed man or woman would enter or leave through the wide portal.

The temple itself had the form of a pyramid built of blocks of golden sandstone. Images of a cat-headed goddess were carved into the stones beside the entrance. It was an impressive edifice, although by no means the largest or most grandiose temple within the City of the Gods. D'Molay approached at a good walk, threading his way through the throngs that filled the streets of the Temple District with practiced ease. He had bathed, changed into fresh clothing including a magnificent cloak of a dark burgundy color that accentuated his eyes, and groomed his beard and mustache to a punctilious neatness. As he turned in toward the temple doors, one of the guards stepped forward to meet him.

"Good afternoon, Zar-Ka." D'Molay smiled pleasantly and brought the ivory kill-stone out of his pocket.

"Do you presume to know me, Hu-Man?" growled the Lion. "Are you certain?"

"You cannot fool me, Zar-Ka. No other Lion has a chipped left incisor or that faint scar on the side of his mouth. Let me in. My business is urgent."

"Har har har!" laughed the other Lion, a rumbling laugh that shook his whole body. "You should know better than to jest with D'Molay, brother. He has been a frequent visitor to our temple, and see, he bears the Plaque of Protection."

"Enter, Friend," laughed Zar-Ka, stepping aside.

D'Molay stepped into the antechamber of the temple. Flourishing his ivory tablet, he walked steadily toward the huge idol of Mafdet at the far end of the room. But before he reached it, two cat-headed priestesses appeared. With a bow and a meow, they led him off to the side, and then behind the idol to a curtained door. They ushered him through it, and into a hallway, lit by lines of flickering iron cressets that stretched off into the distance.

They only walked to the first set of cressets. One of the priestesses held D'Molay's arm and stood with him in the center of the corridor while the other touched one of the cressets in certain spots. A square patch of floor began to sink and in just a few seconds D'Molay was carried down into a shaft that took him deep below the surface temple. As this was the first time anything like this had ever happened to him in the Temple of the Cat Goddess, D'Molay watched it all with calm appreciation. Soon enough he and his escort reached the bottom of the shaft, stepped forward, and then watched the magical rising block lift its way back to the surface.

The feline motif was everywhere. Paintings of cats hung on the corridor walls. Tiles embossed with black cat silhouettes paved the floor. The heavy teak door in front of them had a large cat face carved into the wood. It smiled at D'Molay with emerald eyes. But, the cats portrayed were not ordinary cats; they were cheetahs, leopards, and black panthers. The panther-headed priestess stepped forward and scratched on the wood, uttering a delicate growling noise at the same time, and the door silently swung open. The priestess curtsied and gestured for the man to enter. D'Molay stepped forward and walked into a room all hung and furnished with dark velvet.

"I believe you have something for me," growled the goddess. She sat stiffly on a carved throne of dark basaltic rock. She wore a simple white cotton shift on her slim human body, but she had the head and neck of a black panther.

D'Molay took the Orb of Ra out of his pocket and offered it to the goddess. She purred deep in her throat and the golden ball floated out of his hand, crossing the intervening space. When it reached her, she cupped it in both hands, and it began to emit a golden glow. She held it for a moment, then it floated upward until it reached the highest point in the chamber where it hung, glowing brightly.

"Is there anything else that you require, Goddess?" D'Molay asked.

"Not at this time, Tracker, but you shall be of service to the cat goddesses of Khem many times before you leave the City of the Gods forever. I name you Protector and you have the blessings and good will of the Cats.

"I am pleased that I could serve you, but I am not your servant, Goddess," D'Molay explained. He knew that the gods and goddesses of this realm tended to claim the services of the humans who lived here, and those humans wound up being slaves to their divine masters. "I am a Freeman, and I intend to remain that way."

Mafdet smiled and her fangs gleamed in the golden light. "I value independence," she purred, "and you shall keep yours. It is very catlike of you to insist upon it."

D'Molay felt reassured. He dared then to ask a question. He started to speak, but the goddess interrupted.

"I know what is in your heart, mortal, and the emptiness you feel," she said. "Your void will be filled some day. Never give up hope!"

D'Molay bowed deeply. There was nothing he could say to that, and he felt both comforted and vaguely apprehensive that she could see so deeply into his soul. He remained in his bow until she spoke again.

"You may go. Perhaps we will meet again; perhaps not. Even the gods don't know the future. Again, thank you for daring the Necropolis and rescuing the

Orb. There will be a token of Our appreciation at the exit. You may go."

D'Molay turned and strode from the room. The escort led him back to the rising block, and soon he reached the upper temple. A priestess there gave him a bag of golden coins. He smiled, and headed off for the market-place near the center of the City.

When he left the pyramid three jackal-heads fell in behind him. They were dressed in the half-armor of temple guards. The temple of Anubis was not all that far from the temple of Mafdet. In fact, thousands of people, and animal-heads, roamed through the streets of the Egyptian section. D'Molay noted their presence, but he did not think they would try anything in a crowd. He also saw half a dozen cat-heads in the vicinity, and somehow there were always more cats in sight than dogs.

They hadn't walked far until three more of the servants of Anubis appeared in front of him. D'Molay stopped and his hand fell to the dagger he wore at his waist. "What do you want?" he snapped at them, "I'm in the City now and safe from your interference."

"We are not here to harm you," barked the leader of the second group. "Our master is the divine Anubis, greatest of the gods of Two-fold Land, and he wishes to speak to you. Will you deny the request of a god, mortal?" Every word that came out sounded more menacing than the one before it.Every word that came out sounded more menacing than the one before it.

D'Molay stood facing his interrogators, looking back the way he had come. At the far end of the street he saw a panther-headed priestess watching him. He thought about resisting. Perhaps he could hold off the jackal-heads long enough for help to come. And perhaps not.

He let his hand fall away from his dagger and drift a bit behind his body at hip level. Slowly he moved it back and forth. He could only hope the cat-woman would recognize the gesture as a signal of distress, for when a cat moves its tail from side to side, that means it is irritated and growing angry, just the opposite of what a dog means when it wags its tail.

"I will go with you," D'Molay told the jackal-head. "It would be an honor to meet the great lord Anubis."

"Yes, yes," panted the jackal. "You are honored beyond your worth, but every dog has his day." The leader gestured to the others, and they fell into formation around D'Molay. "Follow me, Hu-Man!"

A jackal-head accompanied D'Molay on each side and three remained behind as they followed the leader, who half-trotted down a wide boulevard leading toward a large pyramid of fine-grained brown Egyptian sandstone.

The apex was a cap of pure gold.

Inside, there was not as much room as one would assume from the size of the massive pyramid. Still, there was one broad hallway that led to huge doors carved from ebony and well guarded by a quartet of jackal-heads dressed in light armor and carrying spears. Beyond that doorway was a

grand staircase that zigzagged from the ground level into the heights above. They climbed its twists and turns for four levels and came to another hallway half the size of the one below. It led to another set of ebony doors. The jackal-heads barked at the guards who replied in short yips of affirmation and then swung the door open.

"Go in, Hu-Man. Prostrate yourself before the Lord Anubis, and wait for him to speak to you."

D'Molay gritted his teeth. He had humbled himself before gods in the past, kneeling, bowing, making arcane gestures, but he had never actually had to prostrate himself. A nudge in the back told him he was expected to enter the god's chamber.

Flames danced above the shallow bronze bowls of four braziers placed in the corners of the large square room. At the far end of the chamber, open sky shone above a railed balcony. Luxurious chairs and couches lined one side of the room and a massive scroll-rack filled most of the other wall. D'Molay stepped in, his eyes searching for the god, but at first he didn't see him. Then two glowing red coals appeared in the air at a level a bit higher than D'Molay's head, and suddenly the god appeared.

Under the gaze of those unblinking eyes D'Molay suddenly felt as if his skin were burning. His knees weakened, and he dropped down upon them. The jackal-headed god smiled a doggy smile, his white fangs gleaming. He stalked forward and towered over D'Molay, less than an arm's length distant.

"Most of my worshippers fall prone upon their faces when seeing me," said the god. His voice had an odd rhythm, like the meandering of the desert wind. It came out as a kind of loud whisper.

D'Molay stared at the floor, tiled with alternate blocks of red and white stone, and held his peace. He resisted the urge to fall face forward and grovel at the god's clawed feet. The silence stretched out for more than a minute.

"Very well, I see that you are no worshipper of mine. That is what I would expect of one who would dare to offend Anubis." The god's curious voice rose and fell in a slithery cadence. "Rise then, Dum-olay!" The god seemed to have some difficulty with the form of D'Molay's name. "I grant you the right to speak freely."

The burning sensation on his skin abated. D'Molay stood up, and found that he was a head shorter than the god. It occurred to him that any mortal would be a head shorter than this deity whenever they met.

Anubis turned his back on D'Molay and stepped toward his balcony. "Come, admire the City with me." D'Molay followed him and stepped out into bright sunlight to look down upon the Egyptian quarter. The temple of Mafdet from which he had come seemed quite small from that height.

The god made an expansive gesture that encompassed all the sights spread out before them. "Magnificent, isn't it?"

"Yes, Lord, I have never seen grander. Not even Paris, City of Light, shone as this place shines." D'Molay wondered what the god was telling him. Surely he had not been summoned to admire the scenery.

"And yet I would reduce this place to cinders and ashes if that would allow me to return to the hot deserts and rich black soil of Khem." The god's voice had dropped to a venomous whisper, and D'Molay realized that this Egyptian Power hated it here. Anubis sounded as if he considered the Land of the Gods to be just a form of exile. D'Molay felt an echo of that same bitterness. It was strange how he had come to the City of the Gods - it was not a place he had ever expected to see, nor had he even known of its existence before he arrived.

D'Molay remained quiet. Though he felt a twinge of sympathy for this uprooted deity, it might not be safe to express it. That might put him in Anubis' power. It would definitely be foolish to disagree with him.

They gazed at the city together for a few moments until Anubis changed the subject. "Tell me how you came to rob the Necropolis of Anubis, mortal. Such feats are rare in this realm. It reminds me of the tomb robbers of the Old Kingdom."

"I scarcely remember it, Lord. It is now all a delirium of shadows and fear and flight. It was as if I were guided by a Higher Power when I found and took the Orb of Ra from its hiding place in the Pits of the Dead."

"That would explain much," Anubis hissed. He glared at D'Molay with such intensity that the man could only glance at his feet and try to keep from shuddering. After a time the god looked away, and D'Molay dared raise his eyes again.

"Tell me, Dum-olay, are you not what is called a Freeman?"

"That is true, Lord."

"And you have no patron god or goddess to watch over and protect you?"

"None, Lord. I have been an errand boy for various gods and goddesses since I came here, but I give my true fealty to none of them."

"And that very independence makes you useful to all of Them." A hint of a snarl entered the susurrus of Anubis' voice. D'Molay simply waited.

"Would you enter my service, Dum-olay?" Anubis asked abruptly. "I could use one such as you, and could make you great in this city."

"I would rather retain my freedom, Lord. No, I say it humbly, but I will not enter your service for more than a single task at a time."

"If I asked it of you, would you return to the Cat's temple and steal the Orb of Ra for me."

D'Molay set his jaw and stared up into the glowing hell-pits that were the eyes of the Egyptian God of the Afterlife. "I am sorry, Lord. I could not do that for you."

Anubis barked at him, an angry clap of thunder that rocked the man back on his heels and made him stagger backwards. "I could take your ka!"

D'Molay felt the moment of crisis was upon him. "You promised me my safety, Lord, before I ever entered your presence. Is the word of a god worth nothing?"

Anubis stared at him angrily, and the sensation of fiery heat returned to his unprotected skin, the same sensation that a hot desert wind would cause. D'Molay raised his eyes and glared back. At that moment he didn't really care what the god could do to him so long as he retained his soul's freedom. They stood posed in a strange tableaux for a few moments; it was the god who looked away.

"Go then, Dum-olay! I see that you will be of no use to me, yet none may doubt that Anubis' word is his bond. See that you never come to my attention again, or you shall surely regret it." He made a dismissive gesture.

D'Molay silently turned and strode back toward the ebony doors of the entrance. As he approached, they silently swung open for him, and as he stepped through, they swung closed behind him.

A single jackal-headed servitor awaited him, a different one. This one was not as tall, and the fur on his head was a dark brown instead of the midnight black of the guards at the door. "Follow me!" barked the guide.

D'Molay followed - down the corridor, down the stairs, through the ground floor of the pyramid, and out a door that was not nearly as grand as the one by which he had entered. Until they left the pyramid behind, D'Molay had not stopped to question his guide, but then his instincts told him that something was wrong.

And at that moment seven other jackal-heads stepped out of hiding places and surrounded him. All of them seemed a bit different from his previous escort. They had brown fur instead of black, leaner bodies. D'Molay stopped, his hand drifting down to his knife.

"What are you doing? Where are you trying to take me? I had Lord Anubis' word that he would not harm me."

"I am not Lord Anubis," sneered the one in the lead. The other eight dog-head guards began to yip as if they were laughing at him. "You will sleep the sleep of the damned in the Necropolis of Anubis this night."

With practiced speed D'Molay drew his dagger and lunged at the leader, catching the beast-man off guard. With animal-like reflexes it flinched away from him, but too slowly. The man's knife opened a long cut in the jackal's head. He fell to the street, yelping in pain.

D'Molay whirled and lashed out at another jackal. The creature of Anubis ducked away from his swing. They all circled around him, obsidian daggers in their hands. Their excited yipping had turned to growls, except for the whimpering of the one D'Molay had felled.

The glittering black blades reminded D'Molay that he also had an obsidian blade, the one that he had found on the table beside him back when the morning was young. Two blades could be a better defense than one. With his left hand he pulled it out of its hiding place in his left boot.

A jackal darted at him from the side. D'Molay targeted him with his metal dagger. The killer dodged, but D'Molay's blade scored it and left a trail of blood droplets flying through the air. D'Molay continued his lunge, stepped to the side, and turned in time to see two more of his assailants leaping at him from behind. They yipped and jumped backwards as his knives lashed out at them. This time he missed by the narrowest of margins.

The seven jackal-heads resumed circling him. D'Molay found himself gasping for breath, moving his head in swift jerks from side to side, trying to watch them all, feinting at one, leaping at another. He had to keep moving his feet, had to keep turning.

The killers were in no hurry. They knew their trade. They knew the human would soon weaken. They much preferred to strike from behind. When he faltered for an even an instant, one would dart in and strike at him. On the fifth such strike they drew blood, a glancing cut through his cloak and across his left shoulder. D'Molay knew the end would come soon.

The deep coughing roar of a lion interrupted their sport. Then a heavy assegai style spear flashed out of the sky and pinned one of the jackal-heads to the ground. The growling of D'Molay's attackers turned to yelps of fear, and suddenly the killers of Anubis were in flight.

Zar-ka and his friend sauntered up. "Ho, Hu-Man, we let you out of our sight, and you go straight to the dogs," laughed the Lion-Man that D'Molay did not know by name.

"I am certainly glad to see you," wheezed D'Molay.

"Sharr-Ni, the priestess, told me that you made the sign of a cat in trouble," Zar-ka explained. "How could we not come for our friend, D'Molay?"

"And what fun it was!" laughed the other, after he recovered his spear. "But perhaps we should be on our way, before the City Guard is attracted to this scene of bloodshed. Those dogs certainly made a lot of noise."

"That would be my fault," said D'Molay as he caught his breath. "They invited me to go quietly with them to the Necropolis, but I declined. And you know how dogs are when they get excited?"

The Lion-Men nodded. "Yes, we know."

The Lions accompanied D'Molay to his house in the Celtic district everyone called the Settlement. As they walked across the City, Zar-ka wondered what D'Molay would do next. "You seem to have made enemies of the followers of Anubis."

"I am always making enemies," said D'Molay, "but I make a lot of friends, too. Perhaps I will go visit a lady I know in the Celtic lands, until Anubis calms down."

"Such a shame!" commented Zar-ka's laughing companion. "You have a natural instinct for trouble, Hu-Man. What fun we could have together if you stay! Would you not enjoy having dour old Zar-ka and myself, Rargra, as your protectors?"

"It would be an honor," D'Molay answered. They had reached the doorway to his house. "But I think I would rather protect myself for now."

Return of the Errant Daughter

By Robert Kassebaum

An Egyptian cat goddess who had betrayed her family lies buried in a crypt beneath the Council Plaza. Her time of punishment finally past, she now faces an uncertain future in the City of the Gods...

"**Y**ou've served your time . . ."

Bast lounged on a triangular granite bench next to a fountain - her favorite fountain - she had presented to the City of the Gods during her last Festival of Cats eleven years ago. It was late afternoon and the blue, clear sky yielded to a warm sun. Bast paid little heed to the comings and goings of the local populace around her. She ignored the various salutations of the parading priests and priestesses; she cast her eyes away from the occasional tradesmen, street vendors, and slaves stopping to quench their thirst; she even disregarded the wishful plops of copper coins being lobbed into the water from passersby.

No, Bast's attention was for the fountain itself. It was the first place she had gone to after her release from prison. She needed to know if the fountain was still there, if it still burbled and frothed, and if the gray marble cat statues still played in the water.

"Ten years trapped in that tomb, with no light, no food, no . . . anything."

Her gaze shifted up to the pinnacle, twelve feet high. A kitten, lying on its back, grappled with a ball of yarn. Water shot out of the ball a foot before falling to splash on the kitten and shower into the first small circular basin. Three little soaked cats chased their tails in the shallow bowl, forcing water to rain down to the next, larger saucer.

"Ten years trapped only with my own thoughts . . ."

Bast looked down at the center of the fountain. Three big cats composed entirely of living stone danced a wet ballet on hind legs, performing lovely pirouettes. Front paws pitched over cat heads as tails spun circular tutus. Water spurted in a hypnotic, rhythmic beat from beneath each cat's carefree spins.

"Ten years of social functions not attended and fashions not worn . . ."

Waterfalls rumbled from the scalloped oval trough into the last pool, thirty feet in diameter, one foot deep. Violent waves caused a fury of activity. Bast's eyes darted to and fro, catching the action. There! A cat scampered, chased by water. Oh! And there! A cat leaped, taking a drink midstream. Over there . . . How delightful.

"Ten years lost in darkness, just like that . . ."

She rolled to a sitting position and rested her arms on her thighs. Bast drooped her head, seeing her feline face reflecting in a small puddle of water. "Why is my heart still burdened?" she murmured her query to the cat head. "I suffered ten years for my crime against Sekhmet. Shouldn't my conscience be clear?" She waited for an answer, but none came.

She blinked for a moment, suddenly realizing Sekhmet's face had taken her place in the mystic waters of the fountain. Then she noticed the golden emblem of Sekhmet at the base of the fountain. Bast scrambled from the bench. "No, no, no!" Bast cried out. Her bare feet slipped on the water-soaked ground. She plummeted down, sloshing to her side. Bast slid in front of a beautifully engraved lioness head - Sekhmet's royal seal - the one she used to mark her property.

Bast's heart sank. "Not my fountain, too."

It was true what the jailer said. "Your temple, properties, and treasury, even your title Cat Goddess are Sekhmet's. All I have for you now, Bast, are the clothes you came in with: this skirt, these three tops, a hip belt . . . and this. A small leather pouch with ten gold coins, as decreed by the Council."

Bast hoped Sekhmet had perhaps overlooked the fountain. Picking herself up, she wiped the grime from her body and looked across the rippling pool. Sekhmet's wavy form glimmered back. "What more do you want from me?" Bast wept. "You have everything now. I have nothing else to give you."

Bast glanced down at her garments. "You want my clothing as well? Fine. Take them!" she exclaimed piteously.

Frustrated, Bast unbuttoned her three ivory tops and flung them in the fountain. She unfastened her pearl and teal striped hip belt, and tangled her cat tail with it. "Ugh," Bast fumed, unraveling the mess. Her long royal blue skirt plunged to the ground unassisted. She gathered her skirt and wadded it with the belt. Bast hurled the heap at the wavering cat head. The splash dissipated Sekhmet's visage.

Bast wiped her eyes. "There, happy now?" Her face contorted with disappointment when Sekhmet's watery shape reformed in the pool. Bast grabbed the leather pouch off the bench. "This too?" She winced, fearing even her gold coins now bore Sekhmet's portrait. "Will everything I accomplished be forgotten as well?" Bast held the pouch over the small waves and loosened the draw-strings. "Will this satisfy you?" But before she released the coins, Bast's pointed ears hearkened to a woman's voice on the wind.

"Hojotoho! Heiaha!"

Bast scanned the sky and spotted a mounted Valkyrie flying close to the ground. She looked like one of the Guardians of the City. They kept law and order and did not like any disruption in the flow of commerce.

Bast marveled at the massive wingspan of the white horse as it approached. It had been at least ten years since she had seen one. The Valkyrie steadily pulled the reins back, and relaxed her weight into the saddle. The stallion whinnied, flapped its long wings forward, slowing itself. Hooves sparked the cobblestones as the rider brought her steed to a halt.

The armored Valkyrie dismounted wielding a golden spear. She slung a round shield over her arm, and led her companion to the fountain. "Come now, Treezh. Refresh yourself," she crooned to her equine, reassuring it with gentle hand strokes down its neck. The winged horse dipped its muzzle into the cool water.

The Valkyrie came to attention. "Hail, great Sekhmet," she greeted, bowing with respect, and continued with concern, "Are you all right? I saw you fall when I passed by. Do you need a healer? You seem . . ." the Valkyrie spied clothes floating in the fountain. ". . . confused."

Bast shut her eyes, frowning. It was bad enough envisioning Sekhmet, but worse to be mistaken for her. She peeked into the pool, and saw Sekhmet's condemning gaze. Bast's hand covered her mouth, attempting to conceal a mournful sob. She fumbled backwards and slumped on a bench. The pouch hit the ground. The echo of spilling coins rang in her ears.

"No, I'll be fine," Bast answered. "I just need a moment to compose myself."

Bast took in the inviting oval face with pale blue eyes, a thin slightly turned up nose, and full lips beneath the winged helmet. Curled blond locks draped casually over the Valkyrie's ornamental metallic breastplate, and the thigh length violet skirt gave a hint of nobility to her ensemble.

A puzzled expression crossed the Valkyrie's face. "You're not Sekhmet, are you."

"Sorry, no," Bast grunted, bending over to rake the coins back into the pouch. "We both have the same golden orange color." She jerked the purse strings tight and rose, facing the Valkyrie. "But that's where the similarities end." She strolled to the fountain and stepped in, ignoring the aerial streams of water that hit her as she fished her soaked clothing out of the pool. She scrutinized the fountain. Now where's that other top? Bast pondered, finger at lip. Ah. Over there.

Exiting the shallow pool, Bast laid out her wet apparel on several benches. She gestured with her hand, magically drying each article of clothing, and began redressing herself. "At least I still have my mystical powers."

The Valkyrie furrowed her blond eyebrows. "Are you and Sekhmet sisters, my lady?"

Bast buttoned her last top. "Sisters? No. I'm her daughter, Bast."

The name seemed familiar to the Valkyrie. Bast . . . Bast . . . she twirled the name in her mind. Her face lit up. "Ah yes," the Valkyrie exclaimed. She thrust her spear towards the Council Chambers; the tip made a wispy hiss. "I was on crowd control ten years ago, during your trial." The Valkyrie reverted back to attention. "A spectacular sight indeed," she added. "Gods and mortals lined the Council halls and maneuvered for the best seat when the great chamber doors opened. Those who did not get in lingered outside, hoping for a glimpse of you. It is a rare event when a god is punished."

"Yes." Bast smoothed her skirt and sat. "The jailer dressed me in an enchanting gray gown, and bestowed dainty manacles to my wrists and ankles," she said with sarcasm, laying her hands on her lap. "He fastened a leather collar around my neck, and led me through the streets on a chain." Bast's trembling eyes met with the Valkyrie's. "My adoring admirers flung stones, rotten fruit and filth. And when the jailer yanked me into the Council Chambers," a soft breeze dried the moisture around her eyes, "All within cheered me with 'Betrayer' and 'Murderer.'"

The Valkryie started. "I-I didn't mean to . . ."

"The so-called trial lasted an hour," Bast interrupted, "because a verdict had already been reached in secrecy." She observed a crowd gathering behind the Valkyrie. "Oh, I defended myself, but to no avail." Her cat face sagged. "Five gods, each proclaimed me guilty. The Council wanted an example and I was it. The Council wanted to make it clear what happens when a god commits a crime against another." Bast veered to the fountain. Her whiskers drenched with tears. "That this is what happens," her hands relaxed, her eyes closed, "when you try to usurp your mother."

The last words spoken weighed heavily on Bast's heart, so much so that the burden seemed to pull at her upper torso. She hunched forward, bare-ly catching herself as she folded in anguish. Tears formed a small puddle at her feet. She looked back at her mother's image in the fountain.

"Why mother?" Bast wailed at the peering amber eyes. "Why torment me so?" Another tear fell.

"It is not your mother, but you who causes your grief," the Valkyrie consoled. She caressed Bast's furry shoulder with a soothing hand. "I see sorrow's grip on your personage. Delve deep into your heart, Bast." the Valkyrie smiled, "and summon the love you must still have for her."

Bast reached out-stretched finger tips toward the reflection, disturbing the wet image of her mother's eyes. She examined the moist, wavy portrait and beheld her saturated fur face dragging with sadness. The dam of remorse she had built over the years, burst. Bast's hands cupped her cat head and she cried. "I'm sorry mother! So . . . sorry." Then she just sat, totally distraught and let her tears merge with the waters of the fountain. The Valkyrie kept a close vigil, shooing away pesky on-lookers, waiting until Bast gained her composure.

At length the late day sun started to set and the Valkyrie needed to carry on with her air patrol. She circled her forefinger and thumb, inserted them between pursed lips, and blew. The sharp whistle beckoned her winged companion. "You have a second chance, Lady Bast. Use it well."

Bast glanced back at the Valkyrie. "Thank you for your kindness." She realized she had never asked the woman her name, but it mattered little now.

The Valkyrie mounted her stallion and grinned. The twilight horizon spread wide. "Come Treezh, let's fly. Heiaha!" With thundering hooves and an upwards swoosh of feathery wings, both were airborne.

Bast rose and sauntered closer to the fountain. She looked across the shimmering pool and viewed Sekhmet's likeness, still staring back at her. "What shall I do now?" she said quietly to herself, "I have no home to go to and no god would dare take me in."

Unfastening the strings of her pouch, Bast took a gold coin and flipped it high into the fountain. The coin tinged, somersaulting. It arced and plunked with a resounding splash in the upper small basin.

"O Fountain of Cats," Bast beseeched, arms bent up, palms laid flat. "What does the future hold for me?" She did not expect an answer. You made wishes at fountains. Divination was the Oracle's specialty, but an arduous journey to Buddha's Retreat required time and coins and . . .

It grew silent.

The fountain's waters no longer burbled and frothed. Passiveness transformed the pool's surface. Tranquilly mirroring Bast's dilated pupils . . . Gazing into the still water, she saw an orange tabby cat amble towards a gleaming gold door and mew three times. The door opened. A golden lioness plodded forward. She clutched the cat by its scuff with gripping jaws . . .

Bast's blinks broke the vision. Her heart raced. The sudden roar of cascading water filled her cat ears.

The Fountain of Cats had given an answer.

A door. A single door made of solid gold had suddenly appeared in the middle of the fountain. A lioness's head, molded in the center, guarded the entryway and chamber beyond. It displayed a fearsome grimace. Fangs bared, ready to bite any unwary prey. The maw growled forth a tremendous unheard roar, issuing a warning to all who dared approach the doorway that a powerful goddess dwelt within.

Bast traced the outline of the gold figurehead with a finger and admired the details. Curved ears adorned the broad forehead which diminished to a flat triangular nose with cushioned whiskers one either side. Two flawless amber-hued diamonds nestled as eyes - never blinking, always aware.

Bast placed her palm in front of the nostrils. She felt a warm exhalation. The golden doors of the Great Egyptos Pyramid were magical and shaped to the will of its occupant, often reflecting the mood of the god.

Tonight, Sekhmet emulated the lioness. Tonight, a mother knew of her daughter's arrival.

Bast sighed and pushed against the unyielding door. "Mother, please . . ." she whispered.

Silence was the reply.

She knelt to read the engraved hieroglyphs. *"Sekhmet, who dwells in the desert; Sekhmet, who protects pharaoh in battle; She who plagues; She who heals; She, the devourer of evil; She, the all-powerful; Beloved wife of Geb; Cat Goddess."*

Bast straightened, crossing her arms. "Mother. Please. We need to talk," she called out.

Silence.

Four symbols adorned the door, representing family: a falcon, a canine, a lioness, and a pair of *demon's wings.* Demon's wings? Bast thought. *Tenh-Mer? 'Beloved wings of the goddess.' Family?* She frantically searched for her cat effigy on the door. It was not there, nor her brother Set's jackal symbol. They had both been expunged from Sekhmet's listed 'family.'

Bast's fist hammered the door desperately. "Mother please!" she cried out. The figurehead stirred. Its ears laid back. The lion face crinkled, annoyed with the person who dared disturb its peaceful rest. With a yowl, it snapped at Bast. She stumbled back, her body shook.

A loud thump and a sharp click came from the door. Fur rippled down Bast's spine; she knew she was about to face her past. Her tail twitched, her heart battered uneasily.

She focused on the amber diamonds on the door as fear's clawing grip shredded through her soul. The golden door swung open.

Bast wanted to flee, to hide. But it was too late. Sekhmet enthralled her with a predator's gaze. An intangible mouth grasped Bast's neck, lifting her off the floor. She struggled, thrashing her legs, but soon gave up and accepted whatever fate was about to befall.

Sekhmet's spell pulled Bast through the entryway and into a large cavernous chamber beyond the door. She was carried between two rows of evenly spaced elaborate columns, each lit by twin braziers. Flickering flames cast eerie shadows across the chamber. Her mother's conjuration released Bast in front of an empty, dark granite throne on a raised dais. Feline images were etched in its sides, and the curved backrest arched high with an open space at the plush ruby seat, allowing one with a tail to sit comfortably.

Bast stepped froward. "Mother?"

Braziers on either side of the throne erupted. Fires plumed mushroom soot clouds toward the ceiling; the stench of brimstone permeated the air.

Torches flared in discontent on the back and side walls. Sekhmet's turquoise banners fluttered, fanning sweltering air. Bast cowered, trembling. This was not her mother's chambers. No. This was the Inferno - the realm of Sekhmet's banishment. An arid desert wind buffeted past Bast, slamming the gold door behind her. She spiraled at the sound of impact. Her face clogged with dread. Bast's cat ears heard the bitter click of the lock.

She gulped as her mother suddenly appeared on the throne. Sekhmet posed regally. Hands graced the armrests with nobility, whilst a majestic body postured an august adoration to an imposing cat head. An ebony braided mane, laced with splendid gems, draped fur shoulders and dangled behind her. Even Sekhmet's sheer iridescent turquoise gown projected a dignified sanctity.

Bast's eyes shimmered with dew, her chest constricted, and a tear ran slowly down her fur cheek. Her mother's appearance had changed little since the last time she'd seen her so many years ago. Bast smiled, her arms expanded, hands opened. "Mother, I am happy to see - "

But a flicked palm halted Bast's words of glad tidings. A displeased eyebrow heaved upwards on her mother's cat face. Sekhmet's eyes examined Bast. Her lion tail whipped, each crack of the tuft lashed dissent and disapproval.

Her elated reunion soured. Ecstatic hands muddled, sloping to Bast's navel - one on top of the other. The jubilant grin she had offered so proudly skewed. Bast's cat head bowed. "Greetings great Sekhmet."

"I see they let you out of your box, Bast," Sekhmet noted.

"Yes, Mother."

"Now that you are at my doorstep, what am I to do with you?"

"I came to . . . to apologize for my transgressions, Mother," Bast replied. Her eyes upturned slightly.

"Do I still have a daughter, Bast?"

"I-I stand before you now," She replied meekly

"You are a stranger to me this night. It remains to be seen if you are my daughter."

Bast had forgotten how quick her mother was. Within half a heart beat, Sekhmet had bolted off the throne to tower over her.

"A daughter listens to her mother's words of wisdom," Sekhmet continued. "A daughter honors her mother's patience and love, and a daughter . . ." Sekhmet's completion pivoted with contempt. "A daughter does not betray and banish her mother to a foul place."

Bast crumpled to her knees. "Mother, I'm sorry," she lamented.

"You helped Set kill your father and you betrayed everything we stand for!" Sekhmet roared. The shock waves punched Bast into the dais; crackling fissures split the stone floor. "How could you do such horrendous deeds?" Sekhmet languished back onto the throne, easing herself in. "And a simple 'I'm sorry' will not, can not suffice."

Complacency embodied Sekhmet once again. Her throne creaked as she leaned back. Fingers interlaced one another. "Tell me true, Bast," Sekhmet inquired. "It was Set who beguiled you. A spell he cast . . . It rendered you mad . . . Please," her hands unlocked, pleading. "Tell me it was him."

"Oh mother . . . mother," Bast moaned, shaking her head. "I wanted your seat of power. I wanted your title of Cat Goddess. I went to Set. And with his . . . aid . . ." Bast's cat head dipped. Her quivering palms opened. "I had no idea his plan was to kill father, but I am as guilty as he."

"Then you leave me with no recourse, Bast." Now a tear tumbled down Sekhmet's furry face. "There is nothing you can say that will stave off my verdict." Her finger touched the air. A neon flash sparked a opaqued ankh. Ozone choked the chamber. Bast's death loomed.

"Geb," Bast interjected, pausing Sekhmet's spell. "His voice woke me from my ten-year slumber, hours before my release." She stared at the ankh, her oblivion. "He told me I'd served my time. You should have seen his Ka mother. So pure. So radiant." Bast's eyes misted. "I hung my head in shame. His hand graced my chin and gently brought my gaze up. I beheld father once more: his caring face, and he smiled upon me." Her voice collapsed. "Geb forgave me."

Bast rose with dignity. She dusted off her skirt.

"I will not beg for my life, mother" Bast said. "I know my lust for higher power was horribly wrong." She gestured at her pending doom. "And I am truly sorry. Sorry I didn't become the perfect daughter you wanted or deserved." Bast's whiskers pruned. "But know mother, that your ever-prideful kitten loves you dearly. I hoped to renew the last part of the family I ruined." Her teeth clenched. "But if you want to send me to my father in the Underworld, I am ready to go. I only pray that Osiris will graciously grant my passage to Geb's embrace and that one day you will forgive me."

Bast's demeanor quelled, her tone softened. "So, with my last words - She glanced at Sekhmet's amber eyes. "I love you, mother, and I am ready for my final journey if that be your wish." Bast closed her eyes and waited. She felt two warm hands steady her cat head. A tender kiss touched her forehead. Her mother emitted such a harmonious purr that Bast swooned to Sekhmet's caring grasp.

"I never demanded perfection from you," Sekhmet said, returning Bast back to her feet. "I reared you the best I knew how. I tried to allow you to ascend into the goddess you are now." She looked down sorrowfully, "I was too harsh. And Set's temptations too powerful."

"Mother, don't . . ."

"Hush." Sekhmet's fingers lifted Bast's furry chin. "Arrogance blinded me. In my haste, I almost lost what I held dear to my heart. You." Two tears glittered on her furry cheeks. "With blessed waters, I cleanse our past. The scar between us - now healed. Let us reunite, becoming family again." She rubbed her head against Bast's. "And now I see Geb has granted me a second chance." Sekhmet's tears streamed. "To be the mother you always wanted."

Bast hugged her mother. Sobs resonated throughout the chamber as they embraced. Finally Bast heard the words she had so longed to hear. Beautiful words.

"Welcome home, my daughter, welcome home..."

Long Night of a Cat Goddess

By M. Scott Verne

*In the first City of the Gods novel,
Tenh-Mer the succubus helps someone break
into Set's prison. Afterwards she rushes back to
her protector goddess, Sekhmet, hopefully before
her absence is noticed. But what did
Tenh-Mer miss while she was gone?*

*I*t was late at night in the City of the Gods, but the lit windows of temples and the glow of the remaining moon provided light to the ornate metropolis of deities and their servants. As a lone, bat-winged figure appeared over the outer wall of the Egyptos compound, the pink tone of her skin and feminine features were likewise illuminated. Tenh-Mer, the demonic companion of Sekhmet, flew through the air towards the Grand Egyptos Pyramid. Within that pyramid, Horus, one of the main gods of Egyptos, and Sekhmet, the goddess of Cats, were meeting to discuss matters of state. Tenh-Mer hurried, knowing it was best that she return to her place inside before they finished.

Within the pyramid, Sekhmet had been led into the one of the round chambers used for making appeals to the upper tier of the Egyptos leadership. A viewing balcony circled the entire room allowing witnesses or other gods to sit and watch the proceedings. It always reminded Sekhmet of a gladiatorial combat arena. At one end of the chamber was a raised dais where one of the main deities could ask questions or make accusations. Tonight it was Horus who took that position. Sekhmet was pleased to see that no others were in the chamber at this time of night, save a few of Horus' retinue.

She was in the 'pit,' as it was called by those who had pleaded their causes from it. It certainly felt like one, based on the higher position Horus took on the dais in front of her. Sekhmet looked up at him as a beam angled its way across the room, spotlighting her.

Horus cleared his throat and tried to smile benignly in encouragement. "Sekhmet, you have requested the time to lay out concerns about your ongoing battle with your enemies. I have always held you in the highest regard, so please be at ease and tell me what worries you so."

The goddess tried to ignore the irritating bright light as she spoke. "Thank you, Lord Horus. I do appreciate your time and attention. I shall be brief. I'm sad to say that the Canines have gained the upper hand despite our efforts to counter them. Usually their attacks are strictly on us and our allies, but I fear they have changed their tactics and are planning to undermine your leadership and perhaps even manipulate the Council of the Gods itself. I have come to plead for your assistance in this matter, before it is too late to act."

Her words wiped the placid expression from Horus' face. "That's quite a strong accusation, Sekhmet. What proof have you of this grand conspiracy?"

"We have seen Set meeting with other gods outside of the Egyptos Pantheon and we believe he is hiding an army somewhere in the deserts of our lands. He has also been seeking out ancient texts from Earth that deal with prophesies and powers outside of our realm. I'm certain he is planning something bigger than he ever has before. Action needs to be taken quickly to avert some dread event."

Horus' dark round eyes narrowed and his beak lowered as he considered her words. There was silence for a moment as an advisor leaned over and whispered something to him. Finally, the god spoke. "Sekhmet, know that I do pay heed to your warnings, more so than most. However, I cannot restrain other gods on rumors and innuendos brought before me by their enemies. I will keep a close eye upon them, but until they act or we find proof of their plans, there is little else that can be done."

"But Lord Horus - "

Horus held his hand up to stop her. "My wings are bound in this matter, Sekhmet. Without solid proof, I can do nothing, even to a miscreant like Set."

Sekhmet lowered her head. "I see." She wanted to yell and warn him that it might be too late by then, and that they needed to stop Set now, but she knew it would only irritate the elder god.

"You worry too much about the comings and goings of Set and his kin. Let them make the next move, and then you can catch him in the midst of his mischief. That is when you should let the rest of us know of his crimes. Now rise and go. Let your heart be light and your Ka be ever safe. I'm sorry to make this meeting short, but I have another pressing matter. There has been some kind of mystic explosion at the Prison and I must assess the damage and find out if this is an attack or some strange accident."

Sekhmet bowed to him, "Yes, of course Lord Horus. Always your wisdom guides us."

Stepping out of the beam of light, she tried to gather her thoughts. She realized that her efforts today had been largely useless, but at least she had warned him. Perhaps Horus would take some precautions in secret despite his apparent disinterest. It was the only solace she had for her efforts. Sekhmet walked out of the now-empty chamber, Horus and his retinue having quickly left.

As she exited through the large stone archway, her daughter Bast was waiting for her. Bast was a thin, lithe, tabby colored goddess with the head of a cat. They had been at odds for some time, but had reunited as loving mother and daughter recently. Other than her coloring and shorter stature, Bast looked much like her mother. She wore a light blue Egyptian style skirt with a white fabric belt and a matching vest. Her feet and arms were bare, save for the golden bracelets she had on each arm. Her striped tail waved expectantly.

"Mother, did you have any luck with Horus?"

Sekhmet smiled wanly. "Not really. He will wait, probably until it is too late to do anything. I think the hierarchy too easily forgets the dangers that Set and his ilk have rained upon us in the past." Her black braided hair shook with frustration as she answered her daughter. "Did you hear about an explosion at the Prison?"

"No. But I did see many guards running in that direction. I wondered what that was all about. What should we do next?" Bast asked, while she rubbed her fur covered face against Sekhmet's shoulder in an effort to console her.

Sekhmet hugged her daughter. "I'm sure we'll hear more about whatever happened at the Prison soon enough. For now, we go home. Tomorrow I'll see if I can find more solid evidence to draw others to our cause."

"You tried, Mother. That's all you can do," Bast replied as she pulled back and looked at Sekhmet face-to-face.

"Thank you for accompanying me."

"Of course, Mother. We are all in peril and it gave me the excuse to spend some time with you. But now I need to go back to my temple in Egyptos. Come with me?"

Sekhmet shook her head. "I'd like to, but Horus wants evidence and I have to find some."

Bast bowed slightly. "Very well. I'll see you in a few weeks when I return."

"I'll await your return, my daughter." She gave Bast a quick hug and the two of them parted ways.

Sekhmet walked across the grand lobby of the pyramid and up the stairs to her own private rooms. Despite her best efforts, she could not stop dwelling upon the day's events and her suspicions about Set's plans. Arriving at the golden door to her rooms, Sekhmet absent-mindedly pulled the latch and walked in, lost in her thoughts.

Entering the darkened room, she ignored the booming sound as the door closed behind her. She headed towards her throne across the stone floor, the light from twin braziers casting long flickering shadows from the two rows of ornate columns that ran the length of the chamber. It was then she noticed something was missing. "Tenh-Mer?" She was attuned to the emotional energy that the young demoness generated and could tell that Tenh-Mer was not in the immediate area, even though she was supposed to be.

The cat goddess stepped up to her throne. She was about to take her seat when she noticed a small kitten nestled in the corner of the stone chair. "You didn't get there by yourself," she said, picking up the kitten and sitting down.

She held the kitten close. "So where did Tenh-Mer go?" Sekhmet asked the tiny cat. Had it been a little older, it might well have been able to give her an answer, but none was forthcoming. The kitten curled up on Sekhmet's lap as the goddess sighed, leaned back in her throne and closed her eyes for a few moments, trying to forget the day's events.

A short while later, a shaft of light briefly appeared on the floor as the entrance door was opened and then quietly closed. The familiar sound of small hooves could be heard.

"Tenh-Mer. Come here," Sekhmet spoke into the darkened chamber.

"Sekhmet? Oh, hello..." a nervous voice replied from the darkness.

"Where have you been and what have you been up to?" There was a pause as Tenh-Mer walked across the darkened chamber and into the light nearer the throne. Her petite, winged figure came into Sekhmet's view. In the torchlight, her bright pink skin almost seemed to glow. Usually Tenh-

Mer was virtually naked, but tonight she wore a long white shirt that was obviously on backwards, along with a black leather belt around her waist that made the shirt look like a very short dress. Her long black curly hair cascaded down on either side of her face and along the front of the shirt, making its presence all the more obvious. "And why are you wearing that?" Sekhmet asked.

"Well . . . it was cold and I was trying to stay warm." Tenh-Mer dropped to her knees at the foot of the throne and bowed down, abasing herself before Sekhmet. "I'm so sorry! I . . . I did go out! I, went out for a little flight around the compound."

Sekhmet frowned and her eyebrows furrowed. "I see. Did I not tell you to remain here?"

"Yes. You did, my goddess."

"And why have you disobeyed me Tenh-Mer?"

"I... Just to stretch my wings. I felt so cooped up. I had to get out and feel the air rush over me. I had to fly, so I wouldn't forget how." The guilt and sorrow on her face was obvious.

"I might have guessed. Flying again! We have . . . I have enemies and they would use you to get to me. Do you understand? "

"You mean the Jackal Clan?" She looked up at Sekhmet, concern in her voice. Tehn-Mer's large eyes glistened in the torch light.

"Yes. They . . . Don't change the subject, Tenh-Mer," Sekhmet sighed, redirecting her words before the conversation drifted. "Where did you go on this flight of yours?"

Tenh-Mer paused for a second. "Nowhere really. I just flew around the compound and past the walls."

Sekhmet twitched an ear. "Did you see the explosion at the Prison?"

"Explosion? Oh, there was a flash of light at one of the buildings! It looked like some kind of spell or something."

"You didn't have anything to do with that, did you?"

"Me? No, how could I? You know I don't have those kinds of powers." Tenh-Mer was glad her answer was the truth. The flash she had seen happened before she and D'Molay even reached the Prison.

"Hmm . . . I wonder sometimes," Sekhmet replied. She was aware that Tenh-Mer's only magical power was a permanent spell of attraction and that it was working right now, muting the irritation she should feel toward her dependent. Even though the two of them had been together for a long time, there was no resisting being attracted to Tenh-Mer. "Oh, I'm too tired for this, and it's hard to stay mad at you for any length of time. Just promise me you'll stay out of trouble and keep away from Set and Anubis. Those dogs are out for blood and I don't want it to be yours."

"I promise, Sekhmet. Why can't they just leave everyone alone? Why do they always have to be conquering and killing all the time?" Tenh-Mer's luminous green eyes looked up at Sekhmet expectantly.

"It is their nature, I suppose. That's why we must be careful. We cat deities are the only obstacles to their goal of total conquest. They would just as soon kill us as talk to us. It is our duty to keep them at bay."

"Will the other gods help stop the jackals?"

Sekhmet touched Tenh-Mer's cheek and then stood up. "Perhaps in time. It's been a long day. I'm going to bed. I suggest you do the same." Sekhmet stood up, turned and strolled down the torch lit hallway that suddenly appeared in the wall behind the throne.

"I will," Tenh-Mer called, as she watched her goddess disappear down the hallway

Sekhmet realized she had far more to worry about then the comings and goings of a flighty demoness. Events were beginning to spin out of control. Whatever had happened at the Prison tonight was only a tiny skirmish in a greater ongoing battle. A shiver of fear went up Sekhmet's spine as she walked towards her bed chamber.

Tenh-Mer picked up the kitten that had been left on the throne then followed down the hallway until only the clip-clopping of her cloven hooves could be heard in the darkness.

Wanted: Mordecai

By Jay Allen Sanford

*Like Tenh-Mer, Mordecai is another flying servant, but he works for
Namtar the Slaver god. Unlike Tenh-Mer, Moredeci is one of the less savory
denizens of the City. In this tale, we discover he has a hidden talent.*

Somehow, Mordecai always suspected that his would be an ignoble end.
Feeling frightened and pathetic -- and fatally exposed -- he crouched
trembling atop the open gazebo framework, attempting to use his too-
small leathery gray wings to hide himself from the chaos and cacophony
exploding all around him.

By air, he was embattled by militarized cherubs and screeching harpies;
from below and from adjacent structures, bloodthirsty citizens hurled
stones and spears at him, some already sharpening their knives in antici-
pation of his fall.

Worse -- or rather worst -- he was in the bullseye crosshairs of no less a god than Apollo himself, enraged and firing arrows up at him from the sidewalk, half-again the size of the nearby humans, having puffed himself up several feet in order to increase the firing range and accuracy of his death-tipped arrows.

Oh, and now yon approached several armor-bound City Guardians on winged horses, each bearing their flame-throwing spears at the ready to strike him down, apparently the like-minded aim of nearly every living being in the City of the Gods.

"Should not have left my cave this day, no I should not," he whimpered quietly to himself. "None to help me, none to save me. All hate me." This was not entirely a revelation to the bat-like creature, known and disliked by most everyone but his dual masters (and perhaps even by them) as a lowly kidnapper, notorious for his (perfectly legal) role in local slave acquisition.

But the bat had never been attacked like this, not in the City, where he was usually allowed unfettered entry and exit, at least around the Slave District, thanks to being vouched for by the goddess he served, Lamasthu.

Modecai's new (and perhaps only) friend Kaman knew the bat would be brought down any moment, and that he held the creature's only hope of survival. But what about the risk of exposure? "If only," he moaned, "it weren't for that damnable song!"

Few could have guessed that Mordecai's dank, hidden cave, on the far side of the great lake within the Mayan realm, was actually home to the most breathtaking, haunting, and beautiful music never heard by any other living being.

When not "acquiring" and making dusk deliveries of unbonded slaves to Namtar at the Slavers' Temple, Mordecai dedicated his endeavors to recreating the sounds, beats, and rhythms that he still recalled from his long-ago lifetime in Babylon. As a human priest whose musicianship was once as inspirational as it was devotional, music had been Mordecai's blessing, his skill, his benediction, and (at least until the events of earlier that day), his salvation.

What's more, he owned or at least had acquired, more than enough tools to bring that music to life once again, here in this far-flung land so improbably occupied by all manner of gods, monsters, and men.

The number of stolen instruments littering the huge open cavern had become nearly uncountable: lyres, harps, pipes, drums, reeds, flutes, bells, rattles, sistrums, and all manner of stringed instruments, some fashioned many worlds away from this one. And Mordecai had played them all. Though his fingers were nearly stubby as a gargoyle's paw, the bat's claws were actually quite lithe, filed down and smoothed each day with his teeth and utilized like precisely attenuated finger-picks.

Being ambidextrous as well (an apparent boon courtesy of the goddess who'd transformed him into her service), the wretched looking thing was actually an accomplished musician of utterly unguessed (and unheard) virtuosity! One whose custom-groomed fingers could play nearly any instrument ever conceived.

Mordecai had in fact been building his own unique, magnificent instrument, fashioning it from the cave itself. The construction, which he called a stalactapipe organ, had transformed the hanging stalactites into a sort of large-scale piano-like lithophone. Sounds were achieved by mechanisms that tapped rows of ancient stalactites of varying sizes, using solenoid-actuated leather-bound mallets in order to produce the rumbling tones.

Years had been spent using his claws and diamond-hard fangs to shave down appropriate stalactites to produce specific notes. He then rope-cabled a mallet to each stalactite, activating the strike-pads with a keyboard consisting of gutstrings that he pulled, stroked, and plucked, much like a harp or a lyre. With the action powered by pumps and pistons operated by his nearly tireless feet, the sublime-sounding result was essentially a gargantuan string-controlled organ, carved out from the very womb of his desolate mountain home.

On this morning, Mordecai's musical cave had rung and rumbled to a song he'd heard in his head for so long that he couldn't remember its name or composer. He just knew that, every time he played the tune, the sound pleased his oversized furry ears which, while acutely pained by loud noises, were conversely refined, even sophisticated, when it came to music.

Sitting comfortably on sand-filled seats along the street curb adjacent to the Jolly Rajah, across from an open plaza, was a band of street minstrels, all of them human. Calling themselves the Outways, their impromptu ensemble was usually comprised of anywhere from two to five musicians, playing pipes, lute, lyre, and various other popular instruments deemed most likely to result in their donation trays being filled with currency.

The bandleader Kaman looked barely out of his teens, with longish blonde hair flowing wildly about sharply chiseled features. Small, lithe, and muscular, evident even beneath the voluminous robe he usually wore for street performing, he played many instruments, but favored a stringed gourd quite similar to the guitars he'd once mastered on his own home-world, a place and time known to very few who dwelled within the City.

Kaman (if he had a last name, none seemed to know it) was a Freeman, one who made it a point to always carry the medallion emblem saying so, given to him by the City Council shortly after his arrival in the City of the Gods. He'd been granted the favored status of someone undeclared to any deity or master in return for his assistance in forever closing the unstable entrance portal that last year had delivered him -- and several more troublesome travelers -- to the City.

Even the most all-knowing of gods would probably be surprised to learn just which Earth era had hosted the staging ground of Kaman's contentious youth. Mainly because the general consensus was that there were no men native to that apocalyptic epoch of ruined cities and sentient animals, let alone a solitary boy. The Chinese, Egyptian, African, Babylonian, Indian, Norse, Mayan, and Greco-Roman gods and goddesses all had -- or rather would have -- ample cause to abandon that time and place. The humans had manufactured their own god, only to be destroyed by its uncontrollable power. Of what use were deities of old in such a hopeless, desiccated place?

Other musicians would come and go, including the occasional non-human pipe-playing satyr, each of them receiving an equal percentage of the income derived from passing the collection bowl among sidewalk watchers and passersby. On this day, the band consisted of Kaman, a frequent string-playing collaborator (accompanied, as always, by his two beloved canines), a red-draped visitor whose large stringed instrument required him to hold his hand high in the air to reach its frets, and a preternaturally accomplished whistle player who was already preparing to pack up his seat and instrument to return home.

Kaman found their proceeds were greatest when they performed under the arched entranceway adjacent to the Jolly Rajah, essentially the hub of this neighborhood of ill repute teeming with competing musicians, snake charmers, jesters, jugglers, consorts of questionable gender, and any number of other beggars, all vying for the coin of anyone bold, curious, or foolish enough to approach.

When sunset skewed the neighborhood's disposition rapidly from mildly disreputable to decidedly felonious, the band was playing its final number. Flying adjacent to the large open concourse near the tavern and a nearby abandoned temple, Mordecai heard something that he at first mistook for his "secret sound," a singsong voice (not his own) that he often heard in his head.

He soon realized that, no, this magnificent sound came from outside his substantial ears; this was the sound of music.

Intrigued by what he heard, Mordecai deviated from his normal City Guardian-approved route, to swoop down the alleyways in pursuit of the music as it grew louder and closer. On sighting the Outways, he came abruptly to a landing directly in front of Kaman and his compatriots, just as they were blowing out and putting away their instruments.

"Very good you are," the bat practically hissed, long unaccustomed to the niceties of civil introductions and social interaction. "Want to hear more. Now."

Kaman looked the man-sized creature up and down with distrustful eyes. "I know you, don't I? Aren't you that slavemonger everyone hates, the one who abducts and delivers innocent wanderers to the Temple?"

"True, yes. Hated, perhaps. Do not know innocent."

"Why, you're one of the most despised creatures in all the realms! The only being I've ever heard held in less esteem is that quarrelsome fellow Merlin, the one banished for his treacherous conjurations."

Even as Kaman spoke, Mordecai picked up a lyre and began lightly plucking on it. Out came the same lilting tune the bat had been practicing from his distant memory that morning on the stalactapipe organ in his cave. The other players had already moved on (had fled, actually; the bat had that effect on people), leaving only Kaman to witness the impromptu and unlikely guest performance.

Kaman was astonished by the bat's skill and tone. He noticed the creature strumming and picking notes on the lyre with surprisingly nimble fingers, using its thin and durable-looking whittled claws in a way that reminded him of the guitar picks he once owned aplenty, pity such outland ephemera was so scarce here in the City.

"You're very accomplished," Kaman marveled, his voice now tinged with both wonder and respect (two things Mordecai encountered so rarely that he did not recognize them as such). "Tell me; were you once a man, bat?"

"Yesss," whispered Mordecai, still not taking his eyes of the lyre as he played. "Now, I bat man."

The tune sparked within Kaman a budding recollection that only increased his curiosity about the musical creature. "I think I know that song. In my world, it's an ancient standard of sorts. I remember my folks left me their record collection, and I played them on an old wind-up machine I found in the rubble of a shop. That song was on one of the albums."

"Albums?" asked Mordecai, glancing back again at Kaman before picking up a set of pipes. Kaman was even further astonished when the bat put it to his leathery lips, commencing to produce some of the most mellifluous, divine music the Freeman had ever been graced to hear.

Suddenly, just down the cobblestone sidewalk, the duo noticed the valkyrie Geirronul, a City Guardian well-known to both Mordecai and Kaman as a particularly just and honest constable. She was walking abreast of her winged horse and moving in the opposite direction, affixing a set of printed posters along the pathway and handing copies to passersby, all of whom seemed intrigued by their contents.

Kaman could see that each sheet featured an accurate rendering of Mordecai, accompanied by the announcement "Wanted: Dead, Alive, or Enchanted. By order of Apollo, For Egregious Crimes Against Existence."

Beneath the illustration appeared a larger and even more ominous inscription (if such were possible): "Reward 3,000 Gold."

None of this was missed by Mordecai, whose first thought was of the goddess Lamasthu. Who knows what punishment she'd mete out for having been so ignobled by her servant's oh-so-public shame and notoriety?

Between frightened whimpers, the bat looked to Kaman with pleading eyes. "What is?! Why? Apollo has not authority to command my death, does he? Why would he so do?"

"I don't know," returned Kaman thoughtfully, "but he's an elemental force to be reckoned with, even back where I come from. When my own ancestors finally succeeded in their longstanding mission, to ascend the heavenly realms, they did so in Apollo's name, in his tribute and service."

"Apollo mission," worried Mordecai, glancing back at Geirronul and the lengthening row of Wanted posters now lining the boulevard. "Mission to kill Mordecai."

In approximately that same instant, all who walked along the boulevard were turning their heads to stare at the bat, then at the reward poster, and then the bat again. At the same moment, several bow-bearing cherubs were descending from the sky. And then Apollo's own unmistakably thunderous voice could be heard immediately behind them, shouting.

Mordecai's attempted flight only carried him as far as the roof of a concourse gazebo before he was inundated on all sides by creatures and objects that flew at him with unmistakably deadly intent.

Apollo led the aerial assault of his minion cherubs from the ground, having enlarged his physical size well above the mortal throng. This rapid-growth "trick," while perhaps tiring and unimpressive to peers who knew him well, nonetheless tended to enthrall (and frighten!) both tourists and libidinous witnesses at ground level who thrilled to peer up Apollo's scanty tunic, at the otherwise undraped progenitor of a thousand pregnancies.

But more disconcerting for Mordecai were the harpies flinging their stringy bodies at him, gnashing razor-lined teeth at his exposed flesh. Like Lamasthu, Mordecai always had an affinity and fondness for the winged beasties, and had never run afoul of one. Truth to tell, he once attempted to mate with a harpy, seeing the similarly-built creatures as his most likely procreation, even a damned thing can want for companionship. But his unrefined attempt at harpy courtship had failed, mainly due to physical incompatibilities. And now, the only thing these harpies wanted of him was a large enough chunk of his corpse to drop at the feet of Apollo, to collect the lavish reward.

With all this going on, Kaman found himself a mere bystander to the tumult, looking up at the epically one-sided battle with a mixture of relief that he wasn't targeted and concern for a creature he'd long thought loathsome, but who had challenged his perception with such musical sensitivity and mastery.

Just down the winding boulevard, Kaman spotted the City Guardian Geirronul, who seemed fully aware of the nearby melee but was still posting the "wanted" notices.

"May I trouble you with a query?"

"Trouble is my duty," the valkyrie replied with an authoritative tone.

"What Crime Against Existence has the bat creature committed?

"You haven't heard?" Geirronul replied, genuinely surprised. "Apollo's flying soldiers heard the bat at his cave while patrolling the great lake earlier today, using some unknown device to either reproduce or perform the most forbidden song on this side of existence! To so much as hum this terrible tune is to invite the pain of torture and death."

"A song?!" Kaman asked, astonished. "But I understand Apollo is a deity entirely devoted to music, paid tribute by countless paeans of the Greeks and Romans! He's a master musician himself, and has proved so in countless musical contests, using the magical lyre made for him by Hermes, has he not?"

"It was just such a battle of the bandolas that caused the song to be outlawed," Geirronul said gravely. "Apollo once competed with one of his own sons, Cinyras. He badgered the youth for months, demanding he prove his prowess and display at least an apprentice mastership of that which has long ruled Apollo's own life. Music."

"Ah so," recalled Kaman. "The son lost that contest, correct?"

"Yes, and in humiliation and resentment, the boy took his own life. The song was subsequently declared forbidden by the grieving god. Rather than look inward and bear the blame he deserved to shoulder, he instead cast the rhythmic composition as the true instigator of his son's death."

With this understanding came an unshakable inner resolution within Kaman to help the poor besieged man-bat. Any creature with such a transcendent affinity for music couldn't possibly be all hideous and evil. Appearances notwithstanding.

Kaman withdrew from his travel kit a small oblong box, about the size of a shoe, holding it firmly with one hand while he waved the other in front of what looked like a hexagonal jewel embedded on its face.

It had been some time since he last wielded the device within the city limits. Only he knew the full power and capabilities of the technologically advanced relic from another world, and its secret was worth his very life. Kaman had learned quickly on his arrival that, in a land of magic and omnipotence, high technology was considered a tainted occult deviation not to be trusted. As for anyone who blatantly wielded such technology in or near the City of the Gods, well, few deities would ever suffer such a powerful ungodly rival to live.

But this was an emergency; damn the risk of exposure. And with that resolve, still holding the box, Kaman was no longer standing on the boulevard sidewalk. Instead, he was perched upon the selfsame gazebo roof on which Mordecai was pleading to all who'd listen (that is, nobody) to spare his life.

"How come you here?" Mordecai gasped.

"The box," answered Kaman. "It comes from another place long ago, or rather far ahead. It can relocate anyone who touches it and thinks of a destination, transporting them bodily to any known place desired."

"Talk not more!" Mordecai fairly shouted, grabbing the exposed side of the box just as an arrow grazed his head, painfully nicking a small piece of his ear clean off. "Use box NOW! We escape!"

"From your lips to the ears of a sympathetic god," said Kaman.

Back at Mordecai's stone cavern hideaway, the bat eventually calmed down enough to grant his rare (in fact, first) visitor a tour of his massive musical repository, including a demonstration of the majestic stalactapipe organ that left Kaman speechless and near to tears.

Finally regaining his voice, Kaman advised, "Now that you know the music can be heard by fliers nearby, you'd best not play that forbidden song any more!"

"Yesss, but they not find cave. Hidden, it is, and the whole mountain sings."

"Indeed, the hills are alive." After sharing a hastily cobbled meal of blind cave fish, and edible roots and berries from Kaman's satchel, the two began to talk. Mordecai was still obsessing over the realization that, now, it was he who would be hunted - at least until some appeasement or offering was made to convince Apollo to rescind the bounty. Being a fugitive from divine justice would make him all but useless to both Lamasthu and Namtar.

"Oh, this bad. Very, very bad."

Kaman regretted having no worthy advice for his unlikely new friend. Late that evening, via the box, he returned to his rented flat in The Settlement district of the City of the Gods. He could only hope that nobody had recognized him during his brief appearance on the gazebo with Mordecai.

He'd been sincere in his promises to return to the Mayan Realm for more visits to Mordecai's cave, and future musical jams with the bat's breathtaking collection. But his assurances were ineffective in assuaging the bat's immediate distress, nor could Kaman think of a way to further assist.

Many that night said that a merciless kidnapper such as Mordecai fully deserved to have suffered the most terrible day of his entirely wretched life.

Unfortunately for Mordecai, this was only the first of many days predestined to be far, far worse.

A Coyote's Tale

By Randy Lindsay

Three young Norse gods have a new slave girl, but they are about to cross paths with Coyote, the Native American Trickster god...

Coyote liked traveling through the Cold Lands because the Norse had no sense of humor. They fell so easily to his pranks and reacted in ways that made him laugh. It was always a treat to have business here.

He raised his head and sniffed for any trace of nearby Cold-Landers. Perhaps he would come across one of their females; tall, thin, blonde, and pale. They were everything a woman should not be, but still . . . he found himself attracted to them.

"Coyote."

An image intruded on his mind. Crow snapped his beak in agitation.

"Coyote!" Crow said even louder.

"Yes Crow," Coyote thought back to the wise god.

"Do not be distracted." Crow swiveled his head as he spoke. "Among the People, you are best at scouting hostile lands, but you are irresponsible. Forget about playing tricks on the Norse and do what you were sent to do."

"Of course, Crow." Coyote smiled.

"And most of all. . ." Crow ruffled his feathers in emphasis, "No searching for women."

Coyote stopped smiling. The image of Crow faded from his mind until just a single eye stared at him. Coyote tried to pretend he didn't notice the eye still watching him. How could he get anything done or, more importantly, have any fun, with that eye there.

"Alright Crow," Coyote called out. "I shall not touch any of the Norse women. I promise."

With that, the eye vanished.

It irked Coyote that he had to deny himself the pleasure of any Norse women he might find along the way, just to get rid of Crow. Of course, there was still a chance that women of other races might be found in the Cold Lands. The thought brightened his mood some and he set off towards the border road between the Cold Lands and the City of the Gods.

If anything, or anyone, of interest were to be found, they would be on that road. Not only did it lead to the center of all the lands, but it was the center of all the gods' schemings. Any of the Norse gods coming out of there would be certain to have juicy bits of news that Crow and the others would find of interest. All Coyote needed to do was trick them into telling him. It would be easy as convincing the snow to melt in the spring.

As a god of travel, Coyote moved very quickly when he wanted to. With the power that he called "Feet On Many Places" he ran faster than an arrow flew through the air. Before the crispness of morning had faded, he sat on a hill, looking down at the City of the Gods and the road that left it for the Cold Lands.

He sat until the sun stood overhead.

He sat until his shadow started to grow long. Perhaps Crow was wrong. It didn't appear as if the Norse gods were up to anything at all. Coyote was starting to think that this would not be a wasted trip, when he saw four figures riding along the road, far in the distance.

Coyote's ears drooped as the images of unclad Norse beauties, dancing naked in the forest, fled from his thoughts. He sighed as he rose up to begin his run. The Norse were not the most observant of gods, so Coyote decided to run close behind them.

As soon as he fell into position to follow them he caught a woman scent. She had the clean smell of someone who bathed regularly, which meant she wasn't Norse. Coyote increased the length of his stride until he had a good view of the travelers.

Four of them on horse; three men and one woman. By the looks of her, the woman was a sex slave purchased by the Norse gods while they were in the city. At once, Coyote devised a plan for getting the information that Crow wanted, while having a little fun himself.

He followed the Cold-Landers until nightfall. The lands of the gods were vast. Even with the powers the gods possessed to travel faster than mortals, it often took many days to reach a destination. When the Norse stopped to make camp, Coyote searched the surrounding area for a nice, quiet cave. It took only a little convincing to send the wolf family living there to look for another place to stay for the night. Then Coyote returned to the Norse camp and waited in the dark, listening to their talk.

"She'll make a fine addition to the new castle," said a large Cold-Lander with arms nearly the size of tree trunks. "Better than a hearth fire at keeping a man warm on a cold winter night."

"If it takes the bitter bite of winter to drive you into this woman's arms, then there must be something wrong with your eyesight," said a second Norse god, who then burst into laughter. His laugh rumbled through the air like a buffalo stampede.

"Watch your tongue, Modi," said the third Cold-Lander. "I may not be able to see, but that hasn't made me oblivious to this woman's charms. If Magni needs to be driven into her bed, it isn't because of his lack of vision."

Modi threw his head back and roared with thunderous laughter.

Red-faced, Magni rose to his feet, the muscles in his neck bulging. His breath came out in short bursts like a bull getting ready to charge. Straining muscles caused the tendons in his arms and shoulders to pop.

The laugher stopped. Modi leaped to a battle-ready stance and faced Magni. His eyes were wide and burned with fury, like a warrior who had smoked too much peyote and was willing to battle the world.

"Get on with it," called out the third Cold-Lander. "Once the two of you kill one another, I won't have to share the girl with either of you."

Although his eyes still held their glassy rage, Modi smiled. "Was that your plan all along, Hod? Since you cannot hope to defeat either of us in battle, you will goad us into eliminating one another."

"And take the girl as a prize for having outwitted us?" Magni added.

Now it was Hod's turn to laugh. "I have no need of eyes to see how this will all turn out. The girl and I will share the brand new castle alone. I will make this winter the longest and the coldest ever. She will be glad to return to me and the warmth of my bed."

"How will it look if the god of winter takes refuge behind the walls of a castle?" taunted Magni.

"I am blind," said Hod. "Why should I care how things look?"

Modi reached into a pouch that hung from his belt and pulled forth a drinking horn. He spit into it and said, "Valhalla." The horn filled with golden liquid until it flowed over the top. He raised the horn in the air. "Let us drink to cold winds and warm women."

Magni and Hod pulled out drinking horns of their own and joined Modi. All three drained the contents in moments. Foam and liquid gold spilled over the rims of the drinking horns and down the beards of the Norse. Only Modi left it there, unmolested by hand or sleeve. The anger that burned perpetually in his eyes blazed more fiercely after the drink.

The three Norse gods filled their horns again and continued drinking. Coyote remained in the darkness and waited for what must eventually come to pass. All three of the Cold-Landers had walked out into the dark, many times, to rid themselves of the beer they drank earlier. At last, the slave girl asked to do the same.

Coyote watched to make sure that none of the Norse followed her and then he tracked her through the darkness. When she turned to come back to camp, Coyote stood there in the form of Magni.

"No use waiting until we reach the castle," Coyote said to the girl, in Magni's voice. "Come with me."

Head bowed, the girl walked with slow, hesitant steps. She followed Coyote-Magni through the black of night to the wolf cave. She went where directed and lay down on the soft ground.

Coyote knelt next to her. "Sleep, beautiful one."

With those words, her eyes closed immediately. Coyote admired the shapely form of the woman. The small amount of bright clothing she wore did little to hide her body. She had long dark hair and tan, olive skin. Too bad he had to return to camp before the Cold-Landers became suspicious. Perhaps there would be time later to make the girl's acquaintance.

Coyote took the form of the girl and returned to camp. By then, the Norse gods had lit a campfire and nearly drunk themselves into a stupor. They looked up as the woman-clad trickster walked into camp, but returned to their drinking without giving her any further attention.

The Cold-Landers had provided the girl a sleeping fur. Coyote lay down, with his back to the Norse, and pretended to sleep. He listened to them talk. This was the best time to learn secrets. When warriors gathered around the fire at night, they spoke of brave deeds. Some deeds were in the past, but many were the dream of deeds they dared to plan. No great hero could be happy looking only behind him; each of them lived for the thrill of the next hunt, the next battle, the greatest conquest.

In order to learn the secrets of others, Coyote had endured many punishments; he had suffered thirst in the desert, hunger in the mountains, and even the pain of a knife when he had been captured by the dark god of the Egyptians. But hearing the Cold-Landers tell their stories was a new kind of torture. They spoke only of spilling entrails and raping women. All of the stories were the same. Now Coyote knew why the Norse were in a hurry to die and go to Valhalla.

At last, Hod spoke of something else. "How goes the plan to reseal the border between us and the Mayan Realm?"

"You should not speak of that outside the war councils," said Magni.

"It doesn't sound good for us to war," said Hod. "How can we raid and pillage if the barrier is restored?"

Modi grabbed his war hammer and staggered to his feet. He swung the weapon back and forth a couple of times, nearly falling backwards. Frothing at the mouth, he uttered a few angry words; none of them understandable except for the phrase, "I kill." Then he sneered at Hod and passed out, crumpling on top of his sleeping furs, the war hammer still in his hands.

Hod nodded. "So we will mount a raid on the Afrik Realms like nothing the land of gods has ever seen before. Then we close up the barrier and make merry at their misery. It is a good plan."

"Do not speak of this again," Magni said forcefully. "This will all come to naught if our plans are found out."

"Who will find out?" Hod smiled. "The slave girl? The trees? You worry too much. We are safe within our own lands."

"Perhaps," said Magni. "But with the barrier gone, the fell gods of other lands can travel our realm as well as their agents. We need to be careful." Magni stared across the fire at Hod for a moment, then waved a dismissing hand. "My suspicions are aroused because we are so near to that time."

"What do you mean?"

"The new keep is finished," said Magni. "We travel there even now. Everyone has been told that we built it to protect against Afrik attacks, but you know as well as I that its real purpose is to serve as a strongpoint for the magic which will rebuild the barrier between our realms. It is there that we will sacrifice the totem of power that we took from the Amerind."

"Then why not just build a tower to protect it?" Hod asked. "The focal point cannot be big enough to require an entire keep be built around it."

"True enough," said Magni. "If that were its only purpose a tower would suffice. But it must conceal the build-up of our forces as we prepare for the raid into Afrik lands."

"And should anything go wrong with the barrier ritual," said Hod, "it will be a suitable place to store the loot from the raid, and defend against any Afrik reprisals."

Magni hefted his drinking horn towards Hod. "Your vision is not hampered by your lack of sight. That is indeed the way of it."

The Cold-Landers returned to talk of their conquests. They talked until they were overpowered by the mead from their ever-filling horns. First Hod, then Magni, fell back onto their sleeping furs, horns still part way filled.

Coyote lay there and listened. The deep snoring meant there would be no more news gathered until the next day. Not that he needed more. The Norse had said enough. Crow would be very pleased with what Coyote had learned. He could stand up and leave the camp and be well inside his home-land by time the Norse awoke.

But how much happier would Crow be if Coyote returned with the totem of power? That would restore some of the strength that had been stolen from the Amerind lands. The other Amerind gods would have to recognize Coyote as a brave hero. Even Badger would have to honor him. Coyote slept and dreamed of seeing Badger's face snarled in anger and embarrassment.

In the morning, the Norse grumbled themselves awake. Modi spit into his drinking horn and said, "Valhalla." He emptied the horn of mead and then stumbled to his feet.

"Get up," belched Modi. The Norse god gave Coyote a light kick to make sure he wasn't ignored. "Prepare food for us, woman."

Magni nodded in agreement. "Make haste about it."

Coyote slowly stood up, making sure to stretch out his muscles in imaginary stiffness. Then he shuffled over to a bag that Magni pointed to. Coyote took his time sorting through the meager supplies and chose the dried fish, leaving the slightly rancid smelling haunch of meat for later.

The bag contained no bowls, no utensils, and no cooking pot. Coyote laid the fish on the rocks by the fire and searched for a couple of sticks long enough to hold the meal to be cooked.

Coyote motioned toward the drinking horn Magni held in his hand then pointed at the fish by the fire. After a second time, the Cold-Lander gave a puzzled look and handed over the horn. Coyote spitted the fish on the sticks then poured mead on them until the horn was empty. He returned the horn to Magni and placed the fish over the fire.

From the corners of his eyes, Coyote watched the Norse. When none of them were looking in his direction, he reached into the medicine bag he carried at his waist and pulled out two kinds of herbs. The first would make the fish taste better and perhaps convince the Norse to eat more. That meant they would take in more of the second herb, which would make them unable to function as "Men." And without the distraction of arousal the Norse would be more likely to talk about something that interested Coyote.

Just in case the herb alone was not enough, Coyote adjusted his shape to lessen any interest in his current form. He caused his breasts to sag slightly and removed some of the pleasing roundness of the woman's hips.

He waited for the fish to sizzle and served it to the three Cold-Landers.

All of them wolfed down the fish. An occasional grunt served as their praise for the tasty meal. When they finished, they wiped greasy fingers on their shirts and looked for more.

Coyote pretended to pay them no attention. He busied himself with the pack of supplies, making it look as if he were doing something meaningful and slaveworthy. As soon as he closed the pack the Norse readied their horses for the day's travel. Coyote was placed on a pack horse, which was then tethered to Magni's saddle.

Although he listened for more information about the raid, or the plans to rebuild the barrier, the Norse hardly spoke. Without mead to loosen their spirits and their tongues, they rode in silence and kept a wary eye on everything around them.

At midday they stopped. Modi once again ordered Coyote to "Prepare food."

When Coyote opened the pack, the smell from the haunch of meat drifted out. Starving men had eaten worse and fared well enough. And these were no men, but gods. Still, the meat was spoiled enough that, with a little help from a herb in his medicine bag, it should make the rest of the day uncomfortable for them. On top of that he sprinkled the sweet herb which would cover the taste and make them want more. Then he served it to the three of them.

Hod paused when he lifted the meat to his mouth. He sniffed and then wrinkled his nose. "Our supplies did not hold up as well in the south as they do in our frozen lands. This meat is spoiled. We should wait until we reach the keep and eat of the foods in the larder there."

"Don't act like a woman," said Modi. "We are warriors. Drink a horn or two, of mead and the taste won't bother you any more."

"Of course it has no effect on you," said Hod. "You would have to chew it before you could taste how rotten it is. If you want, you can have mine as well."

Modi glared at Hod. Then he stood up, strode over to the blind god, and yanked the meat out of his hands. "Just to show you there is nothing wrong with it, I will."

After a couple of bites, Modi wrinkled his nose. He stopped chewing - until he looked over and saw Magni watching him - then finished the haunch with renewed determination. When he finished he let out a loud, victorious belch.

"Best venison I've had in years," Modi boasted.

The afternoon was more entertaining than the morning. Within an hour of mounting up, Modi began to belch - frequently. He quit watching the road and the countryside around him and instead closed his eyes.

"How is that meat sitting with you?" Hod asked.

"Just as it should," said Modi. "Wish there were -" Modi brought a fist to his mouth as if physical threat might keep his lunch in place. "- were more."

Magni said nothing at all. He rode hunched over and with his mouth clenched tightly. His complexion lacked the green tint that Modi's had.

"What sort of food should we have to celebrate the raid?" Hod smiled. "How about pig? We can roast one over the fire until the fat dribbles out of it. And some of that cheese that you like so well, but smells like a corpse seven days dead."

Modi opened his mouth, but shut it again and gulped.

"Enough," shouted Magni.

Hod smiled.

The four of them finished the trip in silence; except for the clop clop of horses hooves, an occasional bird call, and the sound of Modi retching.

They arrived before sundown. Coyote looked upon the Norse keep. The Cold-Landers had prepared themselves well. It could easily house hundreds of troops, maybe even more. In all of the Amerind lands there stood no structure as large as this; although, Coyote had seen forts and castles and palaces even bigger in other realms.

At the bottom of the hill, a fence surrounded the keep, made of huge, thick logs that had been sharpened to points at the top. Norse warriors patrolled the wall, on what must be a walkway on the inside of it. In front of the wall, they had dug a wide ditch and filled it with water. Coyote noticed something slip into the water as they approached. Something big.

Guards spotted the group approaching and lowered a gate, which then served as a bridge across the ditch. They saluted the three gods.

Magni, Modi, and Hod ignored the guards and rode through the gate. They rode up the hill, then dismounted in front of the keep and handed the reins of their horses to a couple of beardless Cold-Lander boys. Coyote slid off the packhorse and fell into step behind them.

An icy hand reached out, taking Coyote by the arm, and pulled him away. The husky woman holding his arm motioned with her head for Coyote to follow. "Slaves are quartered over here."

"I belong to Magni," Coyote told the woman.

"Of course you do. That means you go where he tells you to go. When he wants you he will call for you. Until then I can find something to keep you useful to the rest of us."

Coyote looked to the three gods to see if any of them would notice, but all were occupied exchanging greetings with their fellow Cold-Landers. Once inside the keep itself, they moved forward to the great hall and Coyote was taken to the back where the slaves and thralls did the menial work.

The Norse keep was similar to many of the Amerind lodges; both had large rooms that were shared by everyone for everything. The Cold-Landers had separated the warriors in the Great Hall from the less noble classes. In sight of so many people, Coyote would have little chance of changing forms without being noticed. Otherwise, it would be easy to return to where the three now prepared for the evening feast.

"Magni will no doubt want to bed you tonight," said the woman. "Some light work will tire you enough to prevent you from putting up too much of a fight when the time comes."

The woman put her hands on her hips as she looked around. Finally, her eyes rested on a butter churn. "This will do. You put your back into it and get the butter ready by sup. Wear these gloves; we don't want those soft hands of yours becoming calloused."

Coyote took the pair of gloves and put them on. The woman watched him until he grabbed the handle of the churn and began to work. He made sure to act as if he knew nothing about the churn. Even when the woman grew irritated and demonstrated the process, he pretended to have difficulty operating the handle. At last the woman threw her hands up in the air and stormed off to direct the women working around the cooking fires.

After a few disgusted glances in his direction, the woman quit paying attention to his fumbling efforts to churn butter. Coyote noticed as an attractive girl hefted a platter laden with fruits to her shoulder and headed towards the great hall. Another platter lay where the girl had picked up the first.

Coyote looked to make sure that he was not being watched, then walked over, picked up the remaining platter and followed the girl. He used the heaping pile of fruit to hide his face from the kitchen staff and the guards along the way.

When he reached the great hall he spotted Magni and set the platter down next to him. Earlier in the day he had used his shape changing ability to make himself less appealing to the lustful gods. Now he perfected the natural charms of the girl whose form he had taken. If the girl had been attractive before, then Coyote went beyond mortal beauty.

"My lord," Coyote said.

Magni gave an appreciative look up and down the length of Coyote's borrowed form. A wry smile formed briefly and then faded. "There is serving to be done. I will call for you later."

"I have brought what was readied," Coyote said, giving Magni a doe-eyed expression. "It will be a few minutes before more can be brought out. When it is, I will return and fetch it. Until then, I had hoped . . . That is, I have heard so much about the prowess of the Norse warriors I thought I might be allowed to stay a moment and look upon the trophies of your victories that you have placed here in this wondrous hall. And maybe that you would favor me with a tale or two of how you obtained these badges of honor."

Magni pulled on his beard. "It will do no harm if you are a few minutes late in returning to the kitchen. Yes, come with me."

Coyote batted his eyelashes at Magni and then turned in fake bashfulness. While he faced away, he looked about the room. At least a dozen brawny Norse warriors were gathered together in groups, drinking and laughing. Among them, Modi hefted a full horn to his lips and drained it in seconds, showing no signs of being bothered by the tainted meat he had eaten earlier in the day.

Magni walked over to a wall with several bear hides tacked to it. The wall held many trophies of war: weapons that were not of Norse manufacture, pieces of armor painted with heraldic devices, and the heads of several fierce beasts.

"Each of these," Magni pointed to the weapons and armor bits, "came from a worthy foe in battle. I took this spear from the Afrik god Kibuka when last we met. A Mayan hero wore this helmet. Until I removed his head."

Magni pulled a sword from the wall and demonstrated the stroke he had used to decapitate his mortal foe. Then he repeated the re-enactment, giving added emphasis to the gore involved.

Coyote looked along the wall for the Amerind totem. Midway along its length, a pedestal sat on the floor, about four feet out from the wall. On the pedestal sat the Amerind totem. The brown and grey statue of Boar looked as if it had been carved from a natural blending of wood and stone. It stood about nine inches high and twelve inches long and, in Coyote's opinion, looked much better than Boar did in person.

Still, Boar was powerful. He represented prosperity, spiritual strength, organization, and fearlessness. The loss of his totem had weakened the Amerinds. If it were sacrificed to reform the barrier between the Norse and their neighbors, that would hurt Coyote's people even more.

Magni continued the trophy tour - in the other direction.

"The story of this trophy must be impressive," said Coyote as he pointed to a Minotaur head that was mounted on the wall near the totem.

Magni gave Coyote a disapproving look. "Know you nothing girl? These are mortal creatures and not even very well trained at that. Tis the immortals that give the greatest challenge."

"It looks quite fierce," said Coyote.

Magni squared his shoulders a bit. "Well, they are fierce. And incredibly strong. I suppose you can't be blamed for being impressed."

The Cold-Lander walked towards the Minotaur head as he launched into the story of how he had helped Modi track down the beast in its lair.

Coyote gave a wide-eyed smile to Magni when he looked towards him. Then he took a brief glance around the room as the Norse god returned to his tale. No one was paying them any attention. Coyote took a step back. He slid his hand towards the pedestal. If he could touch it, he might be able to cover it with a magic that would prevent the others from seeing that he carried it.

"What have you done?" someone shouted from the entrance.

All heads turned towards a white haired man with one eye.

"Grandsire," Magni called out.

Odin pointed directly at Coyote. "Why have you let an enemy into our midst and treat him as a guest?"

Magni looked at Coyote, a confused expression on his face. "Do you mean this slave girl? We bought her at the auction. There is no way that mortal, or god, could fool the auctioneers."

"That is no slave," shouted Odin. "And it is definitely no girl."

Coyote knew that his game was over. He must take the prize and flee.

Magni reached out to grab him, but Coyote ducked below the Norse's hand.

From a crouched position, Coyote leaped, seizing the totem as he sailed over the pedestal. By the time he landed he had changed into his natural form, absorbing the totem into his medicine bag so that he could run on all fours.

Magni dived for him, but landed on the floor behind Coyote with a loud,

"Ooofff."

The Norse warriors were easy enough to evade, despite their numbers; until Coyote broke for the door and Modi stepped in his way.

Foam began to froth from his lips. Already his eyes carried the battle madness he was known for. He clasped a large axe in both hands. Scything the weapon back and forth created a deadly barrier that Coyote chose to go around.

A couple of warriors tossed spears that came closer to hitting Modi than they did to harming Coyote.

Coyote dodged an attack from Modi and dug his back paws into the dirt, ready to leap past, but something grabbed his tail and dragged him backwards. Magni had seized hold of him, his incredible strength making it impossible for Coyote to break free.

Modi hurled himself forward and brought his axe crashing down. To avoid having his hand chopped off, Magni let go of his tail and Coyote shot past the descending blade. Mostly. The end of his tail burned in pain. Better to have lost part of his tail than his head.

Coyote bolted between Modi's legs and sprinted for the doorway.

Odin stood his ground and readied his spear. The spear that never missed when he cast it, but there were too many fellow Norse in the way to allow for a clear shot at the scampering target.

Coyote skirted past a pair of warriors, which left him less than a dozen feet from Odin the Wise. Odin the One-Eyed.

Leaping into the air, Coyote flicked his tail. Blood splattered Odin's face and struck him in the eye. Coyote spoke to his blood, telling it to burn. And then he ran as fast as he could past the Norse god-king.

He ran out of the keep. He ran into the night. He ran until he could hear no sounds of pursuit. Then he climbed to the top of the nearest hill and howled in victory.

Crow would tell him it was foolish to boast while the enemy still pursued you. Coyote did not care. He had outsmarted the Norse, stolen back the totem, and lived to tell everyone about it.

Now that he had the totem in hand, he could return home in triumph. Crow, Boar, and even Badger would all be impressed with his heroic deed. Maybe more so seeing that Coyote had lost the end of his tail in the process. He was sure it would grow back, but not before Coyote had time to flaunt the war wound in front of his friend's noses.

Yes, all would be good when he went home.

And he would, once he visited the slave-girl. A little stopover to celebrate, in the guise of Magni, couldn't hurt anything.

The Serpent's Coil

By Wendall Brown

*Is fate dictated by the gods
or guided by our own hand?*

On wings of the night they surged, faces striped with lances of punishing light flickering intermittently through the leafy canopy overhead. They had no need of mounts; their dark clawed feet made them as surefooted as any jungle born cat. Leaping from ground to bough, at ease as much in the trees as on the ground, the hunting party was relentless in its pace, unfaltering as the jaguars from which they had been bred and twisted into semblance of humanity, scent of nearing prey ever widening in their nostrils.

Their strides ate up the sod, gathering mile upon fetid, rotting mile underneath them, as they closed upon a quarry unknown - but not unknowing.

The pace of the leader, J'aith, was the swiftest, setting a killing pace that approached a form of desperation. She paused, only in the instant of a sharp drawn breath between the leap from one tangled branch of timber to another, to touch the sickly green circlet of jade which coiled ever tighter around her throat.

The circlet was His, his mark, his totem. Her neck bore the embrace of a feathered serpent that constricted with each step away from the Celestial Temple of the Mayan realm. There the god Quetzalcoatl no doubt still raged, shaking in divine paroxysms of wrath, for what had been lost - for what had been taken.

"Return the Eye to me!" he had hissed. "Return it or fall to rot and ruin in the muck!" Casting the circlet from his wrist, the charm had briefly spread feathered wings to fly from throne to temple floor before writhing about J'aith's throat, clutching the beating pulse of her neck with a hiss to echo the sibilance of its Master.

She was Jaguari, of a kind raised up from beasts to hunt and rend at the beck and call of their divine maker. And though He had given her people speech, for this task she had none. With grunts and growls she called to the others then sprang with yellow bared fangs to begin the pursuit. She was the first, the Bitch from which the pack had been whelped. It fell to her to lead. It fell to her to feel the choking grasp of the serpent, to bring the thief to ground and taste his blood, be he godling or man or something in-between.

Quetzalcoatl's promise was as tight and uncompromising as his charm's stone grip. Bring back the Eye of Blood. Return it or fall she must, breathless and cold, forgotten in the tangled roots of trackless jungle that stretched to every horizon of the Mayan realm. As beast she would have neither known nor cared about her fate. As woman - or even the semblance - she had come to know the fear of Death, and more, the longing for Life. To protect such divine gift, she would send the thief's soul fluttering back to his own Maker, or any god that t'would grant him refuge beyond the red and the ruin of his ended days.

There! She spied a track still wet with swirls of a recent desperate compress. The quarry was close. With a snarl, she called to the others. The pace of the hunt would now increase.

The thief paused to take breath, chest heaving with the hot intake of the fetid air, turgid molecules heavy with sweat and miserly in their gifts of relief. He bent over nearly double, pointed icicle of a nose nearly piercing the muck, frost bright cheeks almost comically rosy. To any observer he looked like a rag formed elf, plaything of a fretful child, tossed from snow covered mountaintops to land forgotten on a jungle playground.

A few more gulps of air and he straightened, tall and gangly, wondering for the thousandth time what trick of fateful Urd had threaded him into such a sorry loom. Although a hundred dooms he had previously escaped, each with a smile and wink to that witchy weaver - surely this time she had him fast in her shuttle.

Night had passed into day. But growing light revealed even swampier ground ahead. It would be easier to lose his hunters in that trackless morass. But impossible to tell what quick sands or yet worse perils of nature might lie ahead as the swamp grew deeper. Rising ground to the right promised more solid footing, a path less treacherous, yet also swift passage for those that pursued him. If this was a crossroads, it bore no sign to point the safer path. Was that the faint cackle of Norns that he heard? Or was it the nearing snarls of Jaguari? It hardly mattered which.

Pulling a dark ruby gem from the pouch at his waist, the fabled Eye of

Blood his "employer" so coveted, the thief was reminded again that his present straits were not the work of Urd at all, at least not entirely, but rather the joke of a more accomplished trickster, Loki of the North. Perhaps it was better to be torn limb from limb by the fangs and claws of bestial Jaguari, the thief reflected. Better that than return to Loki with an empty purse. It was said that his tricks could work their painful course across centuries. At least death at the hands of Quetzalcoatl's minions was sure to be both swift and final.

Holding the distilled essence of innumerable lives, the Eye had been fashioned of blood sacrifices offered up through millennia to the Feathered Snake, each bloody knife-fed cup nourishing His insatiable lust for the power of Life and Death. No god himself, but yet no foreigner to the sleights and

trinkets of Magik, the thief studied the gem a moment longer, a twist of a smile slowly forming around the edges of his over-wide lips. Suddenly decided, he retrieved a pin stuck carelessly in the cuff of his green-dyed leather jerkin. Then, pricking a finger, he daintily called forth a single red droplet. Such work as he was about to attempt would require an offering, however meager. He touched the ruby droplet of his blood to the Eye and was not surprised to see it vanish into the dark red depths of the stone as if it had never been.

"You're a hungry one, aren't you love?" The thief giggled. Then, taken by a sudden humor, he tilted his head back to call out. "Cut my threads will you Urd? Try it and you may account to Loki for your weave!" A few bright plumed birds startled to flight as the thief capered a few comical steps forward and back, tracing a path into the swamp, pointy toed boots sucking in and out of the soggy earth. Now reaching down to grasp long grasses and handfuls of the dark damp soil, the thief set swiftly upon some craft, thoughts flying to fingers as nimbly as the flight of Odin's crows. He was not dead yet, the thief mused chuckling, and there was a reason why men and gods still ruled the beasts.

Birds. Feathered eruptions as brightly arrayed as Ix Chel, Lady Rainbow herself. Birds breaking cover perhaps just fifty zaps ahead of the hunting pack. *(Zap: an ancient Mayan unit of measurement, approximately = 1.82 meters)* Surging forward, J'aith's vision narrowed to a tunnel of murky red light, a tunnel connecting only her heaving, springing form, to the quarry at the end of it.

She could taste the thief's blood. The scent of it floated down the tunnel to reach her foam flecked nostrils, spurring hot surges of new vigor to her pumping limbs. As if she needed encouragement, the circlet cut a fraction deeper into her throat. When had her breathing become so labored? How tight must the circlet become before she would not be able to breathe at all? No matter. The thief's life was now measured in such breaths. With her Master's gem in hand, homeward bound, certainly the grip of the circlet would ease, becoming soft as a caress, until at last it would fall from her neck as she tendered the stone into her Master's grateful hand.

The ground was growing soft as she sprinted along the thief's now visible path. She felt herself floating above ground, up the steps of a Ziggurat. She could feel the cooling breezes as she rose, higher and higher, above the jungle floor. At the top of His temple, Quetzalcoatl was waiting for her. His arms were spread wide in welcome, beckoning His favored daughter home towards blessing and reward. Her vision closed upon his left eye, deep set and dark, now taking on the shape and color of a ruby gem. The gem glowed with pride, pride for her and her alone. She was in the tunnel again, floating weightless towards the Eye of Blood. She must follow the tunnel. Follow the tunnel to reach the end! This was her universe. There was nothing else.

Excited cries woke her from reverie as the rest of the pack caught sight of the thief at last. As her vision cleared J'aith could see him bounding through the reeds ahead, smaller than she had imagined, almost childlike, skin dark as earth, form willowy as a reed. The pack now splashed through knee high muck, gaining steadily on the rag dressed creature - for now she could see that it was indeed too small to be human - as it bounded with sticklike spindly legs onto a more solid patch of ground and then onward though a dank pool of swampy waters to reach another hump of drier earth beyond.

Reaching the first solid patch, J'aith gathered her legs under her and sprang, snarling across the intervening dark water, to land crushing the prey beneath her weight. Her jaws flashed downward, gaping and snapping . . . to taste only grass and mud. J'aith shook her head, gasping in confused breath-less rage as, relieved of animation, her quarry revealed itself as naught but a construct of twigs and loam, with grass for hair, torn kerchief for bodkin.

The cries of her fellows reached her again. Tearing her gaze away from the simulacrum's remains, J'aith's fevered vision found a hunter of another kind. Clutching all of her kindred at once in its slick dark coils, a monstrous serpent had risen from its watery lair to lay a deadly grip upon prey of its own. Only by springing across the serpent's pool had J'aith avoided the fate now revealed for her children.

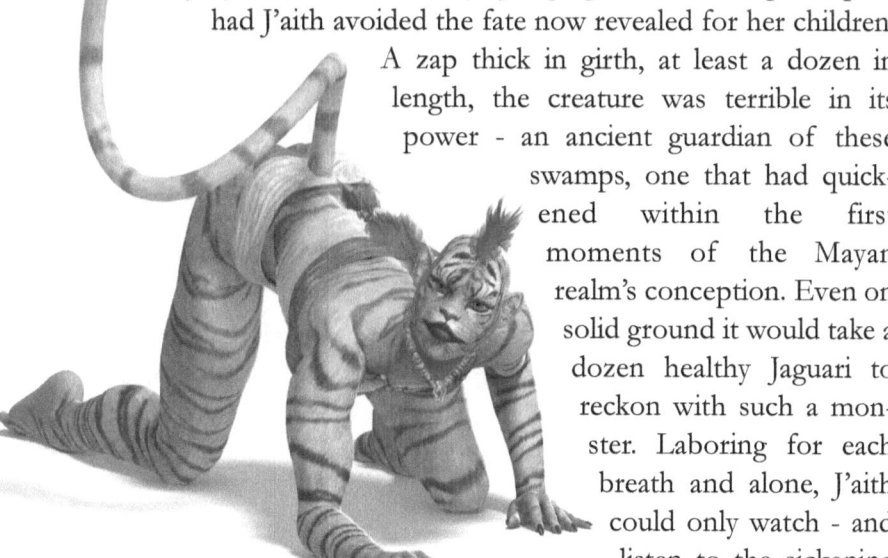

A zap thick in girth, at least a dozen in length, the creature was terrible in its power - an ancient guardian of these swamps, one that had quick-ened within the first moments of the Mayan realm's conception. Even on solid ground it would take a dozen healthy Jaguari to reckon with such a mon-ster. Laboring for each breath and alone, J'aith could only watch - and listen to the sickening

107

crack of bones as the primal anaconda's grip tightened inexorably and her brood's cries faded into sorrowful whimpers. J'aith made no attempt to run away herself. Her strength was near spent and the race would be futile. A behemoth such as this would be able to surge swifter through this muck than she herself could run, at full strength, on hard level earth. The thief's trick had proven as deadly as it was deceitful.

Reaching the edge of the jungle, the thief paused to gaze with admiration at the majestic range forming the border between the Mayan realm and Asgard. Once over the top he would be well and truly beyond Quetzalcoatl's reach. The power of each realm lay chiefly with its own gods and the Feathered Serpent would not dare confrontation with Heimdall and the Aesir who kept a careful watch on all the passes into Odin's realm. Surprised to find a remaining honeycomb and crust of bread in his pouch, the thief wanted only for a horn of mead to form the balance of a decent repast as he contemplated the rigors of the climb now ahead. Even taking it slow, he should still be able to complete the ascent before nightfall.

It had been quite some time since he had heard the last desperate cries of his erstwhile pursuers fading away into a telltale silence. There was no telling, indeed, what fate had overtaken the Jaguari in the swamp while they chased his Blood Doll. He would have to thank Urd, or apologize to all three sisters, for apparently he had mistaken the weft of the Norns' weave entirely. The thief chuckled as his hand found the gemstone in his pouch. And with the Fates as willing mistresses, perhaps he should even revise his plans to hand over the stone so readily to Loki? With a little craft and forethought - who could say? Perhaps the trickster might be persuaded to pay a tenfold ransom for the fruits of this filchery.

Well, mountains did not climb themselves. Stretching out his legs the thief stepped out from under the jungle canopy, eyes seeking for the easiest path upwards.

J'aith could not remember now the time that came before. She knew, as one remembers a fable of youth, that once was a time when breath came easily, when life was not a battle for air, when seconds did not stretch to eternity, thin as the trickle of air that managed, somehow, to still pass in and out between her blue lips.

In this time, the now time, there was only allowance to consider the two warring Ultimates: Air and Adversary. To conquer the Adversary meant Air.

Yet Air must be won to find the Adversary. That was the dictum and the riddle of her life, the only knowledge that mattered, that could matter, as cloudy images of moments lay stranded past bulging eyes that captured light now for one sight alone - the Thief.

J'aith could watch all the moments of her eternity at once: a giant snake head, jaws gaping over her, unable to close, spellbound within a glowing green radiance emanating from J'aith's throat; the behemoth bowing at her feet; a green smear of jungle; J'aith clinging to the rough wet surface of the serpent's back; a gray mountain, topped with white, a strip of brown separating the gray from an area of bright green; an elfin-like figure, nose angling up, knee raised jauntily, centered between the gray and the green.

The last image. It seemed, somehow, important. As important as Air?

Then it could only be . . .

J'aith's awareness snapped back to current time as the Adversary crossed the path of her vision and began to climb the Realm Border. This was what she had waited for. This is why the giant snake had brought her here. Drawing in a huge gasp, J'aith lurched from the trees in pursuit.

Long years ago the thief had learned - the hard way - that nothing was impossible in a world populated by gods. And so when he spied the Jaguari following him up the mountain trail, he was somewhat phlegmatic as he weighed his options. The beast seemed afflicted by some wound or malady, rattling and groaning with the noise of ten ghosts. Still, it was gaining on him - fast enough that it might intercept him before the crest. He would be no match for the creature in a stand up fight. One sweep of claws or a clench of those jaws and he would be done for. Still, no need to force a confrontation early he decided. Better to speed on for now. Perhaps the beast's strength would fail before other measures became necessary.

Take a breath. Take a step. Take a breath. Take a step. The serpent charm, pitiless in its work, had coiled again tighter, as inch by inch J'aith gained on her Adversary. She could not distinguish if the chill she felt was that of Asgard, now just a dozen zaps beyond at the nearing crest, or the chill of Death itself, spreading outward from her throat to still her blood and limbs forever. Looking up, she could see the thief pause and turn. For the first time their eyes met, these pawns on a board drawn by gods. There would be no words and no quarter. There would only be an end.

If he allowed himself, he could almost pity the beast. In its eyes was the light that distinguishes comprehension from the insensate hungers of an animal. It was, in its way, almost human. And so it would die with the knowledge of that which is lost, of striving only to fail - and to fall. Grasping a sturdy rock, one big enough to crush the beast's skull, the thief hurled it downward from the crest, aiming to strike the rattling, huffing hunter square on its head. This stone missed, however, and the laboring Jaguari managed to dodge while still clambering higher, reaching now within an arms length of the thief's position.

A second boulder was grasped and hurled. This one struck the creature's shoulder with a glancing blow. Snarling, it managed yet to lurch another foot upwards, claws reaching within inches of the thief's boot! One more step, and the Jaguari would claim the prize it sought, the life that now sought equally for its own.

The third great rock did its work. Though the beast, surprisingly, did not fall, a great welt of blood began to ooze from its cracked skull as the beast slumped lifeless to embrace the rocks providing it final rest.

The thief sank down on the crest and, after a moment, began to laugh, first at the thought of such a narrow reprieve, and then at the joke of life itself. One step away from the icy grandeur of Asgard, the thief's gaze lingered a moment longer upon his fallen foe. He found himself astonished, as always, by the stillness of death, so swift to follow upon the strife of living.

He noticed a circlet, a work of jade, fashioned as a snake, which now hung loosely about his erstwhile hunter's neck. Perhaps bespeaking that power which had driven this great beast to a height greater than its kindred, it glowed a slumbering green. There was a strange beauty to the charm and beyond its obvious value, it would make a fitting token of all that he had suffered in the Mayan realm, a token to remember this trial, even after the main prize had passed to Loki.

It would not do to leave it. Reaching down, the thief gently lifted the charm and, after a moment's admiration, clasped it around his neck...

Emeralds Also Glitter

By Jefferson P. Swycaffer

Who is the trickiest deity in the City?
There's only one way to find out...
A challenge of the gods!

The streets in the City of Gods were crowded on this market day. Mortal men and women hastened by in all the profuse varieties of humanity, rubbing shoulders with parahumans, monsters, and mythic creatures. Loftier spirits, lordlings and demigods, rode atop palanquins, some enclosed behind brocades, others out in the open sunlight. Their bearers were as likely to be minotaurs, golems, werewolves, or trolls as to be human men.

The highest of the high, of course, never went abroad amidst such a rabble, but remained closeted in their temples, sending servitors or emissaries. But, then, what could the great gods, the high lords of the City's governing council, possibly find to interest them in a public market?

In a street, perhaps narrower and less-often swept clean than most others, by a small fountain-sculpture, a wizened and ancient storyteller unrolled his mat, set out his bowl, and, with a squint at the sun, began to clear his throat in a promising sort of way.

"Would you like to hear a new tale?
A funny story, with a moral.
I promise it has naughty parts.
But it will not scandalize.
Would you like to hear of the River God,
and his feud against the Sun and Sky?
Would you like to hear what Dagon said,
and what rejoinder Odin made?
Let me take you into the temples,
and tell you what the gods have hidden ..."

There was a hint of music in his voice, which was soft at first. But, as a small crowd drew about him to listen -- and some to let a small coin or two drop into the old man's bowl -- his voice lifted, as needed, to carry. He said:

"One day in the City of the Gods, bare-chested Greek Hermes, wing-footed in his messenger's sandals, matched drink for drink with ice-blooded far Norse Loki, while river-shouldered Babylonian Enki, drank likewise. Be warned, some of this tale may be true," the man added.

But, as it happened that morning, Hermes was not wearing his winged sandals, nor did Loki bear spear, sword, shield, armor, or helmet, and, in return courtesy, Enki had assumed a subdued form, mostly manlike, although large and daunting, with his beard softly smoldering.

"Aye, mischief. That is what I say." Loki banged his ale-stein down, spat loudly at the floor, and eyed his companions.

"I have never shown myself averse to a taunt or a scandal," Hermes gave answer. "I only suggest that in moderation there is wisdom, whereas in extremism only sadness lies."

"Your counsel is of cowardice," growled Loki.

"Of reason, prized by philosophers."

"Caution and care. You hesitate when brave gods dare all."

Enki leaned forward as if to interject an opinion, but Loki, blatantly, shoved a hand against the river-god's face and shoved him back. "And no more of you! Your overs-and-unders, your yes-means-no and no-means-yes. I weary of you both! I came to you with a challenge, but all I hear from you is, 'weigh the cost!' But let me tell you this, little godlings: in triumph, there is no cost!"

Enki reached up with his vast, hairy paws, and moved Loki's hand aside. "Yet in defeat, the loss may be great."

"Aye! And we know the answer to that! We do not accept defeat! We succeed! We meet adversity face-to-face, we employ our skills, we connive and we scheme, and we win!"

Hermes coughed lightly into his hand. "I do not think this is going to end well for us." He straightened. "Yet no one calls me a coward, and there is a time for moderation in all things, yes, even moderation itself."

Enki shrugged. "A few months in prison, or in exile. A fine to be paid in gold. A few lashes. Perhaps a brand burned into the skin."

Loki leered at him. "As measured in the balance, against ... Glory!"

Enki and Hermes traded glances, which, slowly, grew into grins. "All right, Loki. All right. What do you have in mind?"

The story-teller sang: "Egyptos god Set, ebon-skinned, jackal-faced, on the Council powerful, mighty of wars, sly in his dealings, magically powerful and heeded by the wise, bides in pyramid-temples tall, by high needles warded. His helmet bears the semblance of his own face; his breastplate is lacquered as black as his own breast. But where a man, e'en a god, bears nipples, his chest plate is set upon with emeralds, twin and cold, and no little of his magic resides in them."

Hermes, Loki, and Enki filed through the streets of noon. They wore only the seemings of ordinary men, so that it might be three messengers, three merchants, or, perhaps, three pickpockets who stepped over puddles of horse-stale, dodged running brats, or waved off the importunings of harlots.

Enki might have been distracted. "We could benefit from more ale." Hermes laughed, and Loki snarled. "There's all the time in eternity for ale," the former murmured, and "Delay is a coward's way of postponing defeat" hissed the latter.

"The women here are plump and sweet." No one of the three had consciously chosen the path that led past the streets and courts where jezebels sang their siren songs. It had simply happened to be the straightest course to the misnamed Nile Gate to the Egyptian Quarter, the name a falsehood as, while a river ran there, it was not the earthly Nile.

"The Council's whips are keen."

"And," Hermes held up a warning hand, "so are the ears of the throng and its idlers."

"Getting cold feet, are you?" sneered Loki.

Hermes shook his head. "I have the courage needed. I only say this: Set is many things. He is a god of war, and of death. He is a god of judgment, with a bent for the prosecutorial. He is a murderer, a thief, a spy, and a deceiver. He is also, in his own way, a god of knowledge and of wisdom. I give you fair warning: he may already know of our intentions."

Loki snorted, and made a great show of spitting into the street. "Then let him tremble in his fear."

He said it, however, in a low voice. With a new grimness, the three stalked along.

<hr>

The story-teller discoursed:

"Have you ever wondered how it is that gods make choices, when choices must be made? How do gods divide a fat loaf, or pour out of a jug? Men cast lots, but never gods! How do they choose? Who wins? Who loses? Who goes first? The gods have their ways! They tie and untie knots; they play at riddles; they watch the sky to see the kind and number of birds that fly into sight, and whether from east or west. At needs, they wrestle ..."

<hr>

Enki went first.

He bypassed the sentry at the first gate with arrent deceit. "I'm on an errand from Pluto." This got him through.

At the second gate, he was more pompous: "Make way for a messenger of Lord Pluto, that great lord known also as Hades, sometimes as Aidoneus or as the Cthonic Zeus." He waved about a staff, and displayed a signet. The guards stepped back on either side.

The third gate was magically warded, and the officers

at attention were equipped with devices of a deep mystical nature: rods, staves, rings, cloaks; shields and swords over which great conjurations had been performed; items of sensitivity so keen as to have smelt a drop of poison in a lake of wine, or the operation of a curse, bane, or malevolence in the midst of a battlefield. Nor were the officers only men: some were jackal-headed, or sphynxine, or otherwise man-beast chimerae.

But their limitations were a part of their nature, for military officers have stolid characters that a trickster-god can take great advantage of. Such men see what they expect to see, and thus, even in the paranoia of their duty, are susceptible to deceit.

"I am expected. My errand is known. Riders were sent ahead. Eh? Ah? No word has been declared to you? Here is my passage -- " He pulled open a scroll, richly indited with colorful blocks of text in hieroglyphic, hieratic, cuneiform, and alphabetic modes. Names were picked out in golden ink, and the many holy names of Set were gold, lined in silver, upon a background of gleaming emerald.

The officers nodded sagely. The riders he'd mentioned had, perhaps, come to grief in their crossing of the countryside. It was high time someone rode forth with a regiment to clean out the nests of bandits and highwaymen. They let Enki in.

Inside at the doors to the temple, the vast pyramid that loomed over the city, Enki's tactics changed, for he knew that this form of misdirection would no longer serve his purposes. Enki strode purposefully forth, then once out of sight seemed to vanish, clouding his presence in a glamour of disinterest. His form and visage altered; his stature dwindled; the colors of his robes grew dull. A magical insipidity lay around him like an aura, and it was only the seeming of a lesser functionary-priest, a lighter of lanterns, a trimmer of candles, a reciter of plain-chants, that went in. The shadows of the immense tomb received him. No one bothered to look at him more than once, and few even granted him a first glance.

From station to station he made his way, with a tottering step, and with the careless and irresolute manner of a man who has performed the same task, day in and day out, for years beyond count. He shuffled along, threading his way among the throngs in the broad corridors, where servitors and slaves dodged out of the path of lords, knights, monstrosities, high priests, and lesser gods themselves. In time, he came to narrower ways, dank and dim, poorly lit by too-few lights, too seldom tended, and in these winding recesses, he was often wholly alone.

The way led downward, far below the level of the city streets. Now he was in the great ancestral tombs, where generations of priests and generals and treasurers and scribes had, properly embalmed and made ready for their crossing of the river to the lands of immortality, been laid to rest in lead-sealed sepulchers. The silence of eons lay about him, and a chill wafted from the stones, an icy sense of numbness as much of the soul and the spirit as of the body.

Ahead, a brighter glow could be seen, and he heard the soft clicking tread of the sentries who patrolled this, the buried keep of Set's treasury, armory, and trove of hidden holdings. Here were gold, gems, coins, bars, decorations, stones, and bangles. Here were the singing swords, the spears of fire, the shields that drew blood. Here were wonders.

Enki now took upon himself a new guise: a jackal-headed man, richly outfitted in the armor of a commander. He drew himself up with hauteur. His strides lengthened and were no longer silent. He rounded the corner and braced the squadron of the guard, jackal-men of the same form as he now bore.

"Attention!" he said, in a voice as inhuman as the baying of a hyena.

The squad snapped to formation.

Enki walked slowly down the length of their rank, in the immemorial, critical pose of an officer making an inspection. He returned the length again, then positioned himself before them.

"Open the doors."

"Yes, Lord," snapped the officer of the guard.

And ... he held out his hand toward Enki, to receive the necessary keys. A very long period of absolute silence followed. Enki's pose began, slowly, inexorably, to wither. He swallowed. His arm twitched. He took half a step to the left.

The squadron fell upon him, a coordinated and skillful attack, weapons reversed so as to strike at him with hilt and haft, for it was certain that the lord of the pyramid would want to have the interrogation of this one. Smitten hip and thigh, shoved low and smashed high, buried beneath the onslaught, it was all that Enki could do to prepare and execute a higher-order effect. He invoked his god-like aura and a personal miracle of translation, bridging time and space, hurling him convulsively away, hundreds of miles over, beneath, and through the lands. He came to rest in a sanctuary temple of his own dedication. Weary, woeful, defeated, and, worse, humiliated, it was there that he lay, slowly healing from his bruises, when a deputation from the Council came to make inquiries regarding an incident in the City.

"For," said the story-teller, "a man may be deceived, as any animal may, as the eyes are weak and the wits are slow. Anyone may, by skill, make himself perceived as what he is not. A god may seem like a man, and, if he hath great knack, a man may, for a brief time, seem like a god. It is no great miracle to persuade a man that he sees what, in truth, he sees not. But it is a different matter wholly to persuade a locked door that it is unlocked!

"Praise the City, and honor to the Council! Enki was tried before a jury of the great, with all due attention to his rights. His excuses were heard. His declarations were given weight. And upon the conclusion of the case, the court decreed only a lesser odium: he was lashed, and cut, and had brands burned upon him; he was made to pay a deep debt of his treasures; he was mired and smeared and befouled with loathsome substances; a scroll of ignominy was read, and posted at each of his temples, and in the temples of his lords and masters.

"Thus humiliated are those who strive to break the wise laws of the Council of the City!"

Loki, not a whit daunted, went next. He whistled and hummed in his overwelming self-satisfaction, and bowed a sardonic farewell to Hermes.

"You would be next ... but I do not plan to fail!" Then he set about the game.

By and large, he followed Enki's course, beguiling his way through the lesser guardians, and avoiding the attention of the greater ones. In the course of his explorations, he came upon the squadron of half-men pacing their sentry-rounds before the locked doors to the treasure hall.

Unlike Enki, Loki had brought a key.

Now, personified as an officer of the watch, he made ceremonious fanfare of his arrival, displayed a writ of entry, and flourished the key. The guards, having once been deceived, stared at him closely, and made a lengthy inspection of the scroll upon which the writ was inscribed. But no one had ever been given cause to impugn Loki's skill as a master-forger. The writ was, grudgingly, acknowledged. The guards, eyes narrowed, lips drawn back from fangs, nostrils distended, stepped away from the door and allowed Loki to approach.

The key, of course, was only a sham, a stage prop. It looked impressive, all of brass, complex and ever-shifting, as much a piece of magic as of clockwork. It wouldn't have opened a tea-chest, let alone the most heavily warded doors in the City. But Loki was, among his many other wicked talents, adept at the recondite art of lock-picking, and the so-called key in his hands housed an assortment of retractable probes. The greatest of human locksmiths might have worked the lock open in an hour; for Loki, it was but the play of a minute, although a long and anxious minute. The guards stared, and began to move closer, encircling Loki. But, at the very moment that their patience had frayed to the point of action, the great lock clicked, clanked, whirred, and chimed. The levers and cogs rotated. The doors swung apart.

Loki saluted the guards with military precision. They, perforce, returned the salute, and took up once more their posts. Loki let himself in to the treasure-suite. Once inside, he gently pushed the doors closed.

The harsh metallic clack of the locks, engaging once more and sealing the doors, was the loudest noise heard that day in the deep catacombs of Set's pyramid-temple. It was a hair-raising sound. But to Loki, it was reassuring, not alarming. He wasn't trapped; he was, rather, secure from interruption.

A lesser thief would have been undone in the next two paces. The corridors within the treasure hall were, naturally, fixed with traps. Loki, with disdainful expertise, stepped over the spring-knives, de-activated the dart projectors, evaded the pitfalls, and slithered about the pressure-points of the deadfalls. An army of men would have been twenty times decimated, but Loki ran the eerie gauntlet of the traps without a single mishap.

At the end of the deadly corridor, the way opened up into the vast, echoing chamber of treasures.

Loki had, in his time, seen plunder.

This trove put to shame every experience he had ever had. Odin's halls boasted not a tenth -- not one part in five hundred! -- of the wealth accumulated here. Zeus, Marduk, Quetzalcoatl, and Shiva, had they pooled their hoards, could not have equaled the half of it.

Coins in gleaming profusion lay scattered amid gems of every hue. Stacked bars of gold supported golden chariots, golden statues, even a golden trireme, complete to the last oar, spar, and sail. Wrought jewelry, statues, tripods, wheels ... Ivory, jade, chalcedony, lapis lazuli, coral ... And everywhere, the buttery light of gold.

Here there was magic. Loki was all but overpowered by the raw scent of it. Devices, cunningly wrought and masterfully enchanted, lay everywhere. He saw: a sword that could cut through a steel anvil; a djinn-charged lamp, good for, not three wishes, but thirty; nine-league boots; adamantine armor; scrolls, charms, curses; a rack of deathcasters, fully charged and ready to slay; time-suspending sarcophagi; crystalline cats that sparkled when stroked; flying brooms. From the greatest and most showy -- a golden dragon, frozen in place, wings outspread, ready to pounce -- to the smallest and most outré -- a poiuyt, or blivet, or "devil's fork," patently self-contradictory and yet undeniably there -- he saw wonders.

Against a wall, in a place of honor, stood Set's armor. Loki approached sidelong, and was obliged to disarm several further traps. When he stood before the outfit, he found himself stirred, all unwilling, by the incomparable artistry of the workmanship.

But ... he had a job to do. Shaking himself free of the inspiration of the moment, he reached out and quietly tweaked loose the two emeralds on the front of the chest plate.

Triumph.

Still ...

Loki raised an eyebrow, and looked back over his shoulder at the treasure. It seemed foolish to leave without carrying away as much as he could cram into his pouch, at very least.

As a man at a dinner-buffet, then, Loki wandered, steps light, smiling to himself. He selected craftily. Those items that were large or weighty, he passed by, but those which were compact, yet possessed of great power, he plucked up. He would hold them for a moment in his hands, while his grin widened: then he would drop them into his pouch. Nor was this any ordinary leathern case, but itself an enchanted carry-all, larger inside than outside by a factor of seventeen.

Greed, with Loki, was something of an art form.

And, just when he thought he might be getting ready to make his departure, he came upon a dinner-buffet in truth: a feast, spread out upon long tables, steaming and fresh, exactly as if served upon that very moment. Loki laughed to himself, and, dragging forth a golden chair, seated himself.

Being a god, he poured a libation. But being a narcissist, he poured it to himself. Then he began to dine. Nor was he disappointed: the display was foreign to his tastes, yet pleasing. It was savory, hot, with a rich variety of spices. There were thin-sliced meats, and wedges of melon; loaves of bread so fine that each bite melted away at the first touch of the tongue; hors d'oeuvres of every imaginable variety. There were goblets of wine: sweet wine, dry wine, sparkling wine.

For only a moment, Loki was in peril of drunkenness. But no; a kind of canny sagacity remained to him, and he moderated his imbibing. It was difficult for him. The wines were surpassing excellent. But, if he bore in his soul no true wisdom, he at least retained a crafty sense of self-preservation. He rose from the table, a bit tiddly, perhaps, but not besotted.

It was when, strolling down yet another avenue of wonders in the seemingly-endless treasure house, that he encountered a troupe of sylphs -- houris, dancing girls, ethereal and dreamlike, suspended in mid-air like sunbeams -- that his self-control was most put to the test.

They were beautiful. Like hummingbirds, like hawks; like the proud figureheads of ships; like courtesans ...

The hunger that now filled Loki's heart was known by another name: lust. He reached out and plucked one -- just one -- of the drifting, lovely figures from the air.

"What is your bidding, my lord?" she said to him.

"I would possess you," he answered, his voice at first a bit tight in his throat.

"Here, my lord? In this place?"

He shrugged. "Good as any other."

The sylph smiled. Her robes were little more than gauze and film. She parted them, and, daintily, with an assumption of modesty, revealed her beauty for him to behold.

Loki put his arms around her, and drew her close. They entered into that union that was ancient when the first god opened his eyes and beheld the starlight.

The problem was, once their lovemaking was done, she would not let go.

The storyteller, using many a circumlocution, and substituting figures of speech, told the tale of the dalliance in a manner befitting the open air of the market. Loki and the sylph were apprehended in flagrante delicto, in the course of re-enacting a primal scene.

"Not for the first time, Loki was caught, not so much having put his neck in a noose, as having stretched his values and trespassed his intimacies. There was some mirth in the court of the lord Set, yet there was also a formal prosecution, and the case came before the Council of the City. As it turned out, Lord Odin, Loki's liege, had, in response to an earlier transgression, been the under signer for Loki's good-behavior, and this parole, now having been broken, placed both Loki and Odin into very uncomfortable situations. Loki, of course, was smirched, physically chastised, publicly disgraced, shorn of the locks of his head, branded, and put on public display for the edification of the citizenry.

"Now, only Hermes remained ..."

But Hermes, it seems, had taken a different approach to the affair. When, earlier, Loki and Enki were first making the rounds of taverns, boasting of what they might accomplish, word had filtered upward to high places. Set had asked Hermes to go on an errand for him: the matter itself was of little import, only that it took Hermes far from the environs of the City. He had been glad to accept two small emeralds for the price of his service.

It was Set, having taken upon himself the guise of Hermes, who had drunk with Enki and Loki. It was Set who had given them the fair warning. "He may already know of our intentions."

Now, with Enki and Loki discommoded, the false Hermes put aside his shape, and grew into the towering form of Set.

"I spoke truly; I am a god of many parts. War-god, death-god, god of judges." He smiled, and his teeth were white and sharp in his muzzle. "But people forget ... I am also a trickster."

The story-teller scooped up his bowl, stood, and backed away into the shadows. No one saw him change his form; he, too, was Set, wearing a contrived body.

It was said to be unfitting for the victor to boast of the victory. But in Set's opinion, the story was too good not to tell. He repeated it, thus, in market-places, street corners, taverns, caravan stations, houses of assignation, tea-rooms, and the shady groves of academies, until he was well assured that it was known, far and wide, to all the lands tributary to the City of the Gods.

Today, he looked into his bowl.

"Four ... Five drachmae ... Six. Six drachmae and change."

The coins would find themselves in a place of honor in his treasure-hall.

Under the Sunset

By Bram Stoker

This story is from Stoker's first published book of fiction in 1881 (also called Under the Sunset). Even in this early work, there is a macabre darkness that later emerges fully in his Dracula novel. Like the next story by Poe, this story also refers to a strange and beautiful country, and a city just beyond the reach of mortals.

Far, far away, there is a beautiful Country which no human eye has ever seen in waking hours. Under the Sunset it lies, where the distant horizon bounds the day, and where the clouds, splendid with light and colour, give a promise of the glory and beauty which encompass it.

Sometimes it is given to us to see it in dreams.

Now and again come, softly, Angels who fan with their great white wings the aching brows, and place cool hands upon the sleeping eyes. Then soars away the spirit of the sleeper. Up from the dimness and murkiness of the night season it springs. Away through the purple clouds it sails. It lies through the vast expanse of light and air. Through the deep blue of heaven's vault it flies; and sweeping over the far-off horizon, rests in the fair Land Under the Sunset.

This Country is like our own Country in many ways. It has men and women, kings and queens, rich and poor; it has houses, and trees, and fields, and birds, and flowers. There is day there and night also; and heat and cold, and sickness and health. The hearts of men and women, and boys and girls, beat as they do here. There are the same sorrows and the same joys; and the same hopes and the same fears.

If a child from that Country was beside a child here you could not tell the difference between them, save that the clothes alone are different. They talk the same language as we do ourselves. They do not know that they are different from us; and we do not know that we are different from them. When they come to us in their dreams we do not know they are strangers; and when we go to their Country in our dreams we seem to be at home. Perhaps this is because good people's homes are in their hearts; and wheresoever they may be they have peace.

The Country Under the Sunset was for long ages a wondrous and pleasant Land. Nothing there was which was not beautiful and sweet and pleasant. It was only when sin came that things there began to lose their perfect beauty. Even now it is a wondrous and pleasant land.

As the sun is strong there, by the sides of every road are planted great trees which spread out their thick branches. So the travellers have shelter as they pass. The milestones are fountains of sweet cold water, so clear and bright that when the wayfarer comes to one he sits down on the carved stone seat beside it and gives a sigh of relief, for he knows that there is rest.

When it is sunset here, it is the middle of the day there. The clouds gather and shade the Land from the great heat. Then for a little while everything goes to sleep.

This sweet, peaceful hour is called the Rest Time.

When it comes the birds stop their singing, and lie close under the wide eaves of the houses, or in the branches of the trees where they join the stems. The fishes stop darting about in the water, and lie close under the stones, with their fins and tails as still as if they were dead. The sheep and the cattle lie under the trees.The men and women get into hammocks slung between trees or under the verandahs of their houses. Then, when the sun has ceased to glare so fiercely and the clouds have melted away, the living things all wake up.

No one can leave the Country Under the Sunset except in one direction. Those who go there in dreams, or who come in dreams to our world, come and go they know not how; but if an inhabitant tries to leave it, he cannot except by one way. If he tries any other way he goes on and on, turning without knowing it, till he comes to the one place where only he can depart. This place is called the Portal, and there the Angels keep guard.

Exactly in the middle of the Country is the palace of the King, and the roads stretch away from it on every side. When the King stands on the top of the tower, which rises to a great height from the middle of his palace, he can look along the roads, which are all quite straight.

They seem to become narrower and narrower as they get further, till at last they are lost altogether in the mere distance.

Round the King's palace are gathered the houses of the great nobles, each being close in proportion to the rank of its owner. Outside these again come the houses of the lesser nobles; and then those of all the other people, getting smaller and smaller as they get further.

Farther off, away towards the Portal, the country gets wilder and wilder. Beyond this there are dense forests and great mountains full of deep caverns, as dark as night. Here wild animals and all cruel things have their home.

Then come bogs and fens and deep shaky morasses, and thick jungles. Then all becomes so wild that the road gets lost altogether.

In the wild places beyond this no man knows what dwells. Some say that the Giants who still exist, live there, and that all poisonous plants there grow. They say that there is a wicked wind there that brings out the seeds of all evil things and scatters them over the earth. Some there are who say

that the same wicked wind brings out also the Diseases and Plagues that there exist. Others say that Famine lives there in the marshes, and that he stalks out when men are wicked - so wicked that the Spirits who guard the land are weeping so bitterly that they do not see him pass.

It is whispered that Death has his kingdom in the Solitudes beyond the marshes, and lives in a castle so awful to look at that no one has ever seen it and lived to tell what it is like. Also it is told that all the evil things that live in the marshes are the disobedient Children of Death who have left their home and cannot find their way back again.

But no man knows where the Castle of King Death is. All men and women, boys and girls, and even little wee children should so live that when they have to enter the Castle and see the grim King, they may not fear to behold his face.

For long, Death and his Children stayed without the Portal and all within was joy.

But there came a time when all was changed. The hearts of men grew cold and hard with pride in their prosperity, and they heeded not the lessons which they had been taught. Then when within there was coldness and indifference and disdain, the Angels on guard saw in the terrors that stood without, the means of punishment and the lesson which could do good.

The good lessons came - as good things very often do - after pain and trial, and they taught much. The story of their coming has a lesson for the wise.

At the Portal two Angels for ever kept watch and guard. These angels were so great and so watchful, and were always so steadfast in their guardianship, that there was only one name for them both. Either or both of them would, if spoken to, have been called by the whole name. One of them knew as much as the other did about anything which could have anything known about it. This was not so strange, for they both knew everything. Their name was Fid-Def.

Fid-Def stood on guard at the Portal. Beside them was a Child-Angel, fairer than the light of the sun. The outline of its beautiful form was so soft that it ever seemed to be melting into the air; it seemed a holy living light.

It did not stand as the other Angels did, but floated up and down and all around. Sometimes it was but a tiny speck, and then it would suddenly, without seeming to be making any change, be bigger than the great Guardian Spirits that were the same for ever.

Fid-Def loved the Child-Angel, and as it rose now and again, they spread their great white wings, and it would sometimes stand on them. Its own beautiful soft wings would gently fan their faces as they turned to speak.

But the Child-Angel never went over the threshold. It looked out into the wilderness beyond; but it never put even the tip of its wing over the Portal.

It was asking questions of Fid-Def, and seemed to want to know what was without, and how all there differed from all within.

The questions and the answers of the Angels were not like our questions and answers, for no speech was needed. The moment a thought occurred of wanting to know anything, the question was asked and the answer given.

But still the question was given by the Child-Angel and answered by Fid-Def; and if we knew the no-language that the Angels were not-speaking we would have heard thus. Fid-Def was talking to Fid-Def:

"Is not Chiaro beautiful?"

"He is very beautiful. He will be a new power in the Land."

Here Chiaro, who was standing with one foot on the plume of Fid-Def's wing, said: "Tell me, Fid-Def, what are those dreadful-looking Beings beyond the Portal?"

Fid-Def answered: "They are Children of King Death. That dreadfullest one of all, enwrapt in gloom, is Skooro, an Evil Spirit."

"How horrible they look!"

"Very horrible, dear Chiaro; and these Children of Death want to pass through the Portal and enter the Land."

Chiaro, at the terrible news, soared up aloft, and got so big that the whole of the Country Under the Sunset was made bright. Soon, however, he grew smaller and smaller till he was only a speck, like the coloured ray seen in a dark room when the sun comes in through a chink. He asked of the Angels of the Portal: "Tell me, Fid-Def, why do the Children of Death want to get in?"

"Because, dear Child, they are wicked, and wish to corrupt the hearts of the dwellers in the Land."

"But tell me, Fid-Def, can they get in? Surely, if the All-Father says, No! they must stay ever without the Land."

After a pause came the answer of the Angels of the Portal: "The All-Father is wiser than even the Angels can conceive. He overthroweth the wicked with their own devices, and he trappeth the hunter in his own snare. The Children of Death when they enter - as they are about to do - shall do much good in the Land, which they wish to harm. For lo! the hearts of the people are corrupt. They have forgotten the lessons which they have been taught. They do not know how thankful they should be for their happy lot, for of sorrow they wot not. Some pain or grief or sadness must be to them, that so they may see the error of their ways."

As they spoke, the Angels wept in sorrow for the misdeeds of the people and the pain they must endure.

The Child-Angel answered in awe: "Then this most horrible Being, too, is to enter the Land. Woe! woe!"

"Dear Child," said the Guardian Spirits, as the Child-Angel crept into their bosoms, "on you devolves a great duty. The Children of Death are about to enter. To you has been entrusted the watching of this dread Being, Skooro. Wheresoever he goeth, there must you be also; and so naught of harm can happen - save only what is intended and allowed."

The Child-Angel, awed by the greatness of the trust, resolved that his duty should be well done. Fid-Def went on: "You must know, dear Child, that without darkness is no fear of the unseen; and not even the darkness of night can fright if there be light within the soul. To the good and pure there is no fear either of the evil things of the earth or of the Powers that are unseen. To you is trusted to guard the pure and true. Skooro will

encompass them with his gloom; but to you is given to steal into their hearts and by your own glorious light to make the gloom of the Child of Death unseen and unknown."

"But from evil-doers - from the wicked, and the ungrateful, and the unforgiving, and the impure, and the untrue you will keep afar off; and so when they look for you to comfort them - as they must ever - they will not see you. They will see only the gloom which your far-off light will make seem darker still, for the shadow will be in their very souls."

"Now, dear Chiaro, become unseen. The time approaches when the Child of Death is to be allowed to enter the Land. He will try to steal in, and we shall let him, for we must work unseen and unknown, that we may do our duty."

Then the Child-Angel faded slowly away, so that no eye - not even the eye of Fid-Def - could see him; and the Guardian Spirits stood as ever beside the Portal.

The Rest Time came; and all was quiet in the Land. When the Children of Death afar off in the marshes saw that nothing was stirring, save that the Angels stood as ever on guard, they determined to make another effort to gain entrance to the Land.

Accordingly they resolved themselves into many parts. Each part took a different form, but all together they moved on towards the Portal. Thus the Children of Death drew a-nigh the threshold of the Land.

On the wings of a passing bird they came; on a cloud that drifted slowly in the sky; in the snakes that crawled on the earth - in the worms, and mice, and moles that crept under it; in the fishes that swam and the insects that flew. By earth and water and air they came.

So without let or hindrance; and in many ways, the Children of Death entered the country Under the Sunset; and from that hour all in that fair Land was changed.

Not all at once did the Children of Death make themselves known. One by one the bolder spirits amongst them, stalking with fell footsteps through the Land, filled all hearts with terror as they came.

However, each and all of them left a lesson for good in the hearts of the dwellers in the Land.

Eleonora: A Fable

By Edgar Allan Poe

First published in 1842, this short piece is regarded by Poe experts as being autobiographical and unusual in the fact that it has a somewhat happy ending. The original edition of the story credits Pyrros as the narrator. We include it in the anthology as Poe describes a place not unlike Realms of the Gods. He also writes of an enticing shining City. Enjoy this often overlooked Poe gem.

I AM come of a race noted for vigor of fancy and ardor of passion. Men have called me mad; but the question is not yet settled, whether madness is or is not the loftiest intelligence -- whether much that is glorious - whether all that is profound -- does not spring from disease of thought -- from moods of mind exalted at the expense of the general intellect. They who dream by day are cognizant of many things which escape those who dream only by night. In their gray visions they obtain glimpses of eternity, and thrill, in awakening, to find that they have been upon the verge of the great secret. In snatches, they learn something of the wisdom which is of good, and more of the mere knowledge which is of evil. They penetrate, however, rudderless or compassless into the vast ocean of the "light ineffable," and again, like the adventures of the Nubian geographer, "agressi sunt mare tenebrarum, quid in eo esset exploraturi." *[They ventured into the sea of darkness, to explore what it might contain.]*

We will say, then, that I am mad. I grant, at least, that there are two distinct conditions of my mental existence -- the condition of a lucid reason, not to be disputed, and belonging to the memory of events forming the first epoch of my life -- and a condition of shadow and doubt, appertaining to the present, and to the recollection of what constitutes the second great era of my being. Therefore, what I shall tell of the earlier period, believe; and to what I may relate of the later time, give only such credit as may seem due, or doubt it altogether, or, if doubt it ye cannot, then play unto its riddle the Oedipus.

She whom I loved in youth, and of whom I now pen calmly and distinctly these remembrances, was the sole daughter of the only sister of my mother long departed. Eleonora was the name of my cousin. We had always dwelled together, beneath a tropical sun, in the Valley of the Many-Colored Grass. No unguided footstep ever came upon that vale; for it lay away up among a range of giant hills that hung beetling around about it, shutting out the sunlight from its sweetest recesses. No path was trodden in its vicinity; and, to reach our happy home, there was need of putting back, with force, the foliage of many thousands of forest trees, and of crushing to death the glories of many millions of fragrant flowers. Thus it was that we lived all alone, knowing nothing of the world without the valley -- I, and my cousin, and her mother.

From the dim regions beyond the mountains at the upper end of our encircled domain, there crept out a narrow and deep river, brighter than all save the eyes of Eleonora; and, winding stealthily about in mazy courses, it passed away, at length, through a shadowy gorge, among hills still dimmer than those whence it had issued. We called it the "River of Silence"; for there seemed to be a hushing influence in its flow. No murmur arose from its bed, and so gently it wandered along, that the pearly pebbles upon which we loved to gaze, far down within its bosom, stirred not at all, but lay in a motionless content, each in its own old station, shining on gloriously forever.

The margin of the river, and of the many dazzling rivulets that glided through devious ways into its channel, as well as the spaces that extended from the margins away down into the depths of the streams until they reached the bed of pebbles at the bottom, -- these spots, not less than the whole surface of the valley, from the river to the mountains that girdled it in, were carpeted all by a soft green grass, thick, short, perfectly even, and vanilla-perfumed, but so besprinkled throughout with the yellow buttercup, the white daisy, the purple violet, and the ruby-red asphodel, that its exceeding beauty spoke to our hearts in loud tones, of the love and of the glory of God.

And, here and there, in groves about this grass, like wildernesses of dreams, sprang up fantastic trees, whose tall slender stems stood not upright, but slanted gracefully toward the light that peered at noon-day into the centre of the valley. Their mark was speckled with the vivid alternate splendor of ebony and silver, and was smoother than all save the cheeks of Eleonora; so that, but for the brilliant green of the huge leaves that spread from their summits in long, tremulous lines, dallying with the Zephyrs, one might have fancied them giant serpents of Syria doing homage to their sovereign the Sun.

Hand in hand about this valley, for fifteen years, roamed I with Eleonora before Love entered within our hearts. It was one evening at the close of the third lustrum of her life, and of the fourth of my own, that we sat, locked in each other's embrace, beneath the serpent-like trees,

and looked down within the water of the River of Silence at our images therein. We spoke no words during the rest of that sweet day, and our words even upon the morrow were tremulous and few. We had drawn the God Eros from that wave, and now we felt that he had enkindled within us the fiery souls of our forefathers. The passions which had for centuries distinguished our race, came thronging with the fancies for which they had been equally noted, and together breathed a delirious bliss over the Valley of the Many-Colored Grass. A change fell upon all things. Strange, brilliant flowers, star-shaped, burn out upon the trees where no flowers had been known before. The tints of the green carpet deepened; and when, one by one, the white daisies shrank away, there sprang up in place of them, ten by ten of the ruby-red asphodel. And life arose in our paths; for the tall flamingo, hitherto unseen, with all gay glowing birds, flaunted his scarlet plumage before us. The golden and silver fish haunted the river, out of the bosom of which issued, little by little, a murmur that swelled, at length, into a lulling melody more divine than that of the harp of Aeolus - sweeter than all save the voice of Eleonora. And now, too, a voluminous cloud, which we had long watched in the regions of Hesper, floated out thence, all gorgeous in crimson and gold, and settling in peace above us, sank, day by day, lower and lower, until its edges rested upon the tops of the mountains, turning all their dimness into magnificence, and shutting us up, as if forever, within a magic prison-house of grandeur and of glory.

The loveliness of Eleonora was that of the Seraphim; but she was a maiden artless and innocent as the brief life she had led among the flowers. No guile disguised the fervor of love which animated her heart, and she examined with me its inmost recesses as we walked together in the Valley of the Many-Colored Grass, and discoursed of the mighty changes which had lately taken place therein.

At length, having spoken one day, in tears, of the last sad change which must befall Humanity, she thenceforward dwelt only upon this one sorrowful theme, interweaving it into all our converse, as, in the songs of the bard of Schiraz, the same images are found occurring, again and again, in every impressive variation of phrase.

She had seen that the finger of Death was upon her bosom -- that, like the ephemeron, she had been made perfect in loveliness only to die; but the terrors of the grave to her lay solely in a consideration which she revealed to me, one evening at twilight, by the banks of the River of Silence. She grieved to think that, having entombed her in the Valley of the Many-

Colored Grass, I would quit forever its happy recesses, transferring the love which now was so passionately her own to some maiden of the outer and everyday world. And, then and there, I threw myself hurriedly at the feet of Eleonora, and offered up a vow, to herself and to Heaven, that I would never bind myself in marriage to any daughter of Earth -- that I would in no manner prove recreant to her dear memory, or to the memory of the devout affection with which she had blessed me. And I called the Mighty Ruler of the Universe to witness the pious solemnity of my vow. And the curse which I invoked of Him and of her, a saint in Helusion should I prove traitorous to that promise, involved a penalty the exceeding great horror of which will not permit me to make record of it here. And the bright eyes of Eleonora grew brighter at my words; and she sighed as if a deadly burden had been taken from her breast; and she trembled and very bitterly wept; but she made acceptance of the vow, (for what was she but a child?) and it made easy to her the bed of her death. And she said to me, not many days afterward, tranquilly dying, that, because of what I had done for the comfort of her spirit she would watch over me in that spirit when departed, and, if so it were permitted her return to me visibly in the watches of the night; but, if this thing were, indeed, beyond the power of the souls in Paradise, that she would, at least, give me frequent indications of her presence, sighing upon me in the evening winds, or filling the air which I breathed with perfume from the censers of the angels. And, with these words upon her lips, she yielded up her innocent life, putting an end to the first epoch of my own.

Thus far I have faithfully said. But as I pass the barrier in Times path, formed by the death of my beloved, and proceed with the second era of my existence, I feel that a shadow gathers over my brain, and I mistrust the perfect sanity of the record. But let me on. -- Years dragged themselves along heavily, and still I dwelled within the Valley of the Many-Colored Grass; but a second change had come upon all things. The star-shaped flowers shrank into the stems of the trees, and appeared no more. The tints of the green carpet faded; and, one by one, the ruby-red asphodels withered away; and there sprang up, in place of them, ten by ten, dark, eye-like violets, that writhed uneasily and were ever encumbered with dew. And Life departed from our paths; for the tall flamingo flaunted no longer his scarlet plumage before us, but flew sadly from the vale into the hills, with all the gay glowing birds that had arrived in his company. And the golden and silver fish swam down through the gorge at the lower end of our domain and bedecked the sweet river never again. And the lulling melody that had been softer than the wind-harp of Aeolus, and more divine than all save the voice of Eleonora, it died little by little away, in murmurs growing lower and lower, until the stream returned, at length, utterly, into the solemnity of its original silence. And then, lastly, the voluminous cloud uprose, and, abandoning the tops of the mountains to the dimness of old, fell back into the regions of Hesper, and took away all its manifold golden and gorgeous glories from the Valley of the Many-Colored Grass.

Yet the promises of Eleonora were not forgotten; for I heard the sounds of the swinging of the censers of the angels; and streams of a holy perfume floated ever and ever about the valley; and at lone hours, when my heart beat heavily, the winds that bathed my brow came unto me laden with soft sighs; and indistinct murmurs filled often the night air, and once -- oh, but once only! I was awakened from a slumber, like the slumber of death, by the pressing of spiritual lips upon my own.

But the void within my heart refused, even thus, to be filled. I longed for the love which had before filled it to overflowing. At length the valley pained me through its memories of Eleonora, and I left it for ever for the vanities and the turbulent triumphs of the world.

I found myself within a strange city, where all things might have served to blot from recollection the sweet dreams I had dreamed so long in the

Valley of the Many-Colored Grass. The pomps and pageantries of a stately court, and the mad clangor of arms, and the radiant loveliness of women, bewildered and intoxicated my brain. But as yet my soul had proved true to its vows, and the indications of the presence of Eleonora were still given me in the silent hours of the night. Suddenly these manifestations they ceased, and the world grew dark before mine eyes, and I stood aghast at the burning thoughts which possessed, at the terrible temptations which beset me; for there came from some far, far distant and unknown land, into the gay court of the king I served, a maiden to whose beauty my whole recreant heart yielded at once -- at whose footstool I bowed down without a struggle, in the most ardent, in the most abject worship of love. What, indeed, was my passion for the young girl of the valley in comparison with the fervor, and the delirium, and the spirit-lifting ecstasy of adoration with which I poured out my whole soul in tears at the feet of the ethereal Ermengarde? -- Oh, bright was the seraph Ermengarde! and in that knowledge I had room for none other. -- Oh, divine was the angel Ermengarde! and as I looked down into the depths of her memorial eyes, I thought only of them -- and of her.

I wedded; -- nor dreaded the curse I had invoked; and its bitterness was not visited upon me. And once -- but once again in the silence of the night; there came through my lattice the soft sighs which had forsaken me; and they modeled themselves into familiar and sweet voice, saying:

"Sleep in peace! -- for the Spirit of Love reigneth and ruleth, and, in taking to thy passionate heart her who is Ermengarde, thou art absolved, for reasons which shall be made known to thee in Heaven, of thy vows unto Eleonora."

Exclusive Excerpt from City of the Gods: Guardian

By M. Scott Verne & Wynn Mercere

An advance look at City of the Gods: Guardian.
Enjoy this sneak peek at the upcoming second novel in the City of the Gods series.

From the top of the dune, D'Molay could see a shape in the distance. "There's something ahead. Could be a palace, maybe a city," he called down to the others.

"Then we should visit and hope they welcome guests," Mazu said as her camel caught up with his. Close behind her came Quan, perched proudly upon his animal like a satrap. As he did at every stop, Quan took the opportunity to voice his opinion about what to do next. He prodded his camel to a stop next to Mazu's and leaned slowly toward her, taking care not to slip from his mount.

"Or we should avoid it, and escape a trap," Quan added.

D'Molay had come to accept the man's inflated ego and contrariness, but had not yet completely schooled himself to ignore it. "We'll never find her if we don't look," he said, mild irritation evident in his voice. "We can get there before nightfall, so let's make for it. I'll keep the lead." D'Molay immediately started down the side of the dune, heading for a flatter run of desert.

"He wants to die first," Quan said, unwinding the colorful scarf wrapped around his head and beating out the dust that had collected on it.

Mazu smiled at her devotee. She enjoyed his personality. She'd never confess it to D'Molay, but she was vastly entertained by Quan's remarks. However, he was wrong in this case. "No, D'Molay's days of wanting to die are behind him," she said.

"If you say so, Lady Mazu," Quan acquiesced. "But if he stirs up a sand beast or a lair of bandits . . . " His worries trailed off as they hurried to catch up with their leader.

After an hour of riding, they could see more. Carved stone columns rose out of the sands among crumbled walls and statues, some canted at odd angles. When they reached several intact buildings on the outskirts, they discovered them to be empty shells. D'Molay's slumped shoulders made his disappointment clear.

"Maybe there are people living in the central region. That's often the case when a city is in retreat," Mazu said, hoping to instill some optimism in the men. D'Molay said nothing, merely urging his camel to continue on, leaving Mazu and Quan to converse about the styling of the abandoned plaza and the obscure designs etched in its paving stones.

The wind blew gusts of sand before them as they traversed the central street of the forgotten town. There was no sign of habitation. As they passed the remains of some larger ruined buildings, they saw a huge crater hundreds of yards across and hundreds of feet deep. Everything within and around the crater looked as if it had been melted by some unimaginable heat, leaving crumbling buildings and debris half-buried in the ever-shifting sands

"Fire dragon nest!" Quan chirped in alarm.

Mazu smiled. "Don't worry. If we meet a fire dragon, I can put him out."

D'Molay began to dismount his camel. "I want to see what's down there." The animal grumbled as it knelt.

"Even the camel thinks he's crazy," Quan muttered. Ignoring him, D'Molay walked on towards the crater's edge as Quan turned to Mazu. "What made that hole?"

"In the early days of the realms, there were many battles. Few pantheons were satisfied with what the Council gave them and often attacked the cities given to others. When peace came, this area was so badly damaged that it was sealed off to use as a place to keep things too dangerous or unwanted."

"Ah, we shouldn't let him go alone then," Quan said.

"More curious now that I've convinced you it's not a dragon's nest?" Mazu teased. "Very well, let's get off and give our rides a rest."

Their camels sat languidly in the heat as the goddess and the fisherman joined the tracker. He stood at the lip of the crater, gazing down at what was once the stairway of some grand building. He was able to descend a section of the broken steps, moving down to where the remains of a partially destroyed statue of a woman lay. The image of Aavi turned into salt flashed through his mind.

Quan broke D'Molay's train of thought. "What are you doing down there?"

D'Molay looked up to see Mazu and Quan looming above him. "I was considering camping in here out of sight for the night, but it's too unstable. One loud snore from Quan and we'd be buried in an avalanche of stone."

Quan folded his arms and lifted his chin high. "I do not snore."

"Yes . . . " Mazu grinned, ambiguous toward which man's statement it affirmed. "I think the buildings we saw as we came into this town seemed safe. Perhaps there are more like them on the way out." They moved on.

A short while later they did find an ancient temple that still had walls and a roof. It was large enough for the three of them - and the camels - and even had an old cooking pit in the center of the floor. D'Molay converted that into a campfire and found two toppled benches that allowed them to sit around it. Quan began to prepare a meal while Mazu used her power to make sure the camels had something to drink. She made water appear in her cupped hands and the animals drank eagerly.

They shared warm tea, dried meat and the last of the crumbled sweet-cake. After dinner, D'Molay kept one eye and ear alertly pointed toward the door while Quan began to nod from the seductive warmth of the fire. Mazu, less paranoid and in no need of mortal rest, preferred to talk.

"Do you sense something out there, D'Molay?"

He downed the last of his now cold tea. "I don't know. With the things we've seen lately everything seems threatening. I still want to know what Circe was doing with all those urns filled with blood."

Mazu tossed a small twig into the fire and looked at him earnestly. "There are some things that cannot be known. We have the antidote and escaped with our lives. We should be thankful for that."

"I know. It's just hard to forget. You didn't see how many urns of blood she had. Hundreds, thousands of them."

"Millions," Quan interjected awkwardly in an attempt to pretend that he hadn't nodded off and was part of the conversation, his head jerking up from where his chin had rested upon his chest.

Mazu picked up the kettle and warmed D'Molay's cup. "However many, there is nothing to be done tonight. Circe's lair is on the other side of the realms. We need to concern ourselves with our current situation."

"Sorry. I know you're right. I just can't stop thinking about it. Where did all that blood come from and what is she doing with it?" Despite his unanswered question, D'Molay went over to his traveling bag and got out his map of the realms, returning and unfolding it to consult with Mazu. "As for our current journey, we don't have much to go on as far as my map is concerned. My visits to the Lost Realm have been rare and I never went too far into it. Based on where we entered, I think we're about here." He pointed to an area of the map beyond the barrier they had passed through and studied the lands nearby. "Isn't Scylla supposed to live along the shoreline of a lake?"

"The dryad didn't mention a lake, just the Anagar swamp. But water clings to water, so it could be near one," Mazu said.

Quan stretched and slapped his thighs in an attempt to wake himself fully. His next words came out in the company of a yawn. "You had to talk of water, didn't you? Now I have to go rid myself of my own."

Mazu smiled at Quan's simple needs as he walked out. She wished D'Molay could set his anxiety aside as easily as her other friend. She eyed his map. "Could the swamp on your map be the same one we seek, but called by a different name?"

"Possibly. I got my information from a guide in Luxor. Maybe Anagar is the word for it in another language."

Suddenly Quan rushed back into the room, arms gesturing frantically toward the darkness outside. "I saw something," he hissed in a loud whisper. "I think they've found us!"

"Who, Quan?' Mazu asked, extending a calming hand to catch one of his flailing arms. D'Molay shot to the door-less frame and melded his body to the wall, peering into the night, listening. He heard nothing, other than the sound of the night wind.

"I'm sure there are men out there!" Quan insisted.

"One way to find out," D'Molay said. He took one step outside but immediately everything felt wrong. He fell into a defensive crouch just in time to miss being hit by a spear that flew into the house and slammed against the back wall. It was almost as if an unseen force had pushed him down, but he had no time to consider how that could be the case.

"Away from the doorway!" D'Molay commanded. Quan and Mazu quickly complied, with Quan being visibly shaken. Mazu, as usual, wore a mask of calm concern.

"You were right, Quan. I wonder what they want," she said as two more spears thudded into the wall and a shout went up from the warriors outside.

"Based on those spears, they want us dead!" Quan said, trying not to hide too obviously behind Mazu's robes.

"Then I will try to change their minds," she decided. Before D'Molay could object, Mazu quickly stepped into the opening. "Cease this saber rattling, we mean you no harm," she said in a loud, strong voice. This offer was met with a new volley of spears.

Quan screamed in horror as their points pierced Mazu and their shafts continued through her body, splattering dark liquid in their wake. Every instinct and experience told D'Molay that Mazu ought to be dead, but still she stood, unaffected by the attack. "Mazu!" he cried out.

She glanced at him for just a second before again addressing whatever waited outside. "Now that we've gotten that out of the way, perhaps we can discuss this reasonably." She took a few more steps forward and moved out of D'Molay's view.

He stared at the spot where Mazu had just stood, seeing only the dark puddles on the floor. Then he came to a sudden realization. "It's not her blood. It's water!" Two more spears flew through the entrance as a spray of additional water followed them in.

"W-water?" Quan sheepishly asked, still in shock from the attack on his beloved Mazu. But the goddess seemed to be fine. D'Molay and Quan could hear her berating their unknown enemies.

"I am not certain which will run out first, my patience or your spears. Where is your leader? Let me speak to him ere I'm forced to drown you all," they heard Mazu say.

D'Molay couldn't resist the urge to lean over and take a peek out of the arched entry. It was almost pitch black outside as the moons had set in the sky, but he could see Mazu in the light from their campfire. Though she was still in the shape of a woman, she had turned completely into clear swirling water, the flicker of the fire making her form glow and shimmer.

"Kill that thing!" came a call from the darkness. At the same time, D'Molay was again inexplicably shoved away from the door into a safer area of the room. Certain he had not imagined the effect twice, he had faith he knew the cause of it. However, that mattered little at the moment, as more spears flew through Mazu to harmlessly bounce off the back wall.

"Thing?" Mazu was yelling. "You dare call me a thing?" D'Molay had rarely seen her so angry, but now, like a churning sea during a storm, she was roiling. Mazu outstretched her liquid arms and they turned into flexible whip-like geysers. The attackers who were charging toward her were blasted off their feet back into the darkness, except for one. He managed to hurtle past Mazu and throw himself through the doorway. The warrior slid along the wet floor, grabbing one of the spears that had been thrown into the house.

D'Molay lunged at the large figure before he even realized it was a minotaur, with a massive bull's head, bulky muscular body and large cloven hooves. D'Molay moved quickly, grabbing the shaft of the man-thing's spear while lunging in with his knife. The minotaur grabbed D'Molay's hand, stopping the knife in mid-thrust. D'Molay felt painful pressure as the creature tried to force him to drop his blade. Unable to bear it, he let go, and the knife hit the floor with a metallic clang. The minotaur then threw D'Molay off as if he were no more than a bag of laundry.

D'Molay flew head first towards the nearby wall, but instead of crashing into it, his progress was oddly slowed, allowing him to lightly thud against it and slide down to the floor. Wasting no time, he rolled up on his feet, grabbing a spear in the process, and readied himself once again for an attack.

The minotaur grunted at him and charged, spear at the ready, like a knight at a joust. D'Molay followed in kind, running to meet him, but at the last second he dropped to the floor and slid, shoving the spear up into the minotaur's gut as he collided with its leg. The minotaur's spear missed D'Molay, scraping the ground and falling out of the creature's grasp. Immediately D'Molay rolled out of the way, his back against the opposite wall. But the minotaur wasn't done, despite having a spear sticking in its torso. The creature spun to face D'Molay again. It grabbed the protruding spear with one hand, pulling it out and pointing it back at him. The minotaur started to advance as blood poured out of its wound.

D'Molay tried to get to one of the other spears lying on the floor, but they were out of reach. The minotaur closed the gap between them and swung out with its massive fist. He dodged the blow, but the creature grabbed him with its other hand. Just then, the minotaur bellowed in pain. Quan had picked up a spear and run it though the creature's gut from the side. The minotaur dropped D'Molay, wheeling on Quan and knocking him off his feet with the shaft of the embedded spear as it swung around. The minotaur bellowed again, taking several staggering steps forward. Quan was frantically crawling away, but before he got too far, the creature stopped moving and fell face forward onto the ground, missing Quan by mere inches.

Seeing Quan was all right, D'Molay lurched across the room to retrieve his knife and headed for the door to see how Mazu was faring. He watched as she continued to drive back any warriors foolish enough to cross her path. She struck them with powerful blasts of water and lashing whips of liquid crystal. Their long coils defied gravity as they remained in the air, sweeping away opponents left and right. Finally the attackers withdrew and the night fell silent. D'Molay walked outside to praise Mazu for her victory. As he approached, she resumed her human form, leaning on her wooden staff, looking exhausted.

"That was amazing," he congratulated, but putting his hand on her shoulder he could feel she was shaking. "Do you need help?"

"Yes. Get me back inside our shelter," she said in a strained voice. As she turned he could tell she was unsteady on her feet. Putting his arm around her waist, D'Molay helped her back inside. Mazu seemed thinner, lighter and more fragile then he'd ever seen her.

"What's the matter? Did they cast some spell on you?" There was deep concern in his voice as they got inside the battered house, out of sight from any who still might be watching.

"My Lady, you saved us!" Quan exclaimed as he came over to them.

"L-let us hope that is the case," she responded weakly as D'Molay helped her sit down by the fire. She looked tired and worn out, the lines on her face more prominent than usual.

"Mazu?" D'Molay asked again. He had never seen her in such a state before.

She gave him a sidelong glance and tried to swallow. "They did nothing, other than force me to use my reserves to keep them back. The effort has drained my life force. I'll recover, but it will take some time." She closed her eyes as though even the effort of answering had taken a toll on her.

"But I've seen you use your powers many times before. Why has this attack weakened you so much?" D'Molay sometimes felt he would never understand the way gods worked. He'd always assumed Mazu was immortal and invulnerable. She gave him a weary look.

"We are in a desert and I am a water goddess. I have been away from life-giving waters for too long. Now I am paying the price." Her voice faded off.

"We need to get you to water as soon as we can!" Quan insisted. "You never should have gone out to fight them," he chided her, the concern in his voice obvious. He then fumbled with the pockets of his coat, retrieving something. "Mistress, I brought you a bottle of the life water. Using it would restore you," he said with an odd hesitancy.

Despite her condition, Mazu gave Quan a harsh glare. "I told you not to pack any of those bottles for this journey, and you disobeyed me?"

Quan was crestfallen, unable to hold her disapproving gaze. "I - I am sorry my goddess. But please, I beg you, for your own sake, please partake of it." Quan prostrated himself before her, his head touching the floor as he slid a blue glass vial topped with a cork toward her. Mazu stared at it disdainfully.

"If Quan brought something that can help you, use it. Isn't it divine providence that it is even here for you to take?"

Mazu's gaze turned from her disobedient servant to D'Molay. "Providence has nothing to do with this, I assure you." He noted a look in her eyes that reminded him that she had lived far longer and knew far more than he might ever learn.

"Please Lady Mazu, you must," Quan added, still not daring to look up from the floor.

D'Molay reached over and picked up the small blue vial, holding it close to his face to see it in detail. The liquid looked clear, perhaps with a trace of lavender and small golden flecks shimmering within it. It seemed more like an oil extract or syrup than water, moving slowly when he tilted the vial.

"What is this?" he asked.

There was a pause, then Mazu sighed. "It is the nectar of the gods. It is used as . . . medicine when needed."

"It is needed. You need it. If we are to continue on this journey, you must take it." D'Molay took the vial and placed it in her hand.

She held the vial tightly. "Should I?" She looked at the two men in front of her, and realizing her responsibility to both of them in this dangerous realm, came to a decision. "Very well. I will take it once again." She opened the vial and drank down its entire contents.

D'Molay saw her hollow cheeks fill out, the color return to her face, and the lines of her face vanish. The age spots on her hands faded and the veins retreated back under her skin, which became smooth once again. Even her hair seemed to become fuller and slightly darker. She frowned when she realized D'Molay was gawking at her.

"I am not a circus attraction. Let me rest now and the nectar will finish its work while I sleep," she said waving the two of them off.

"All right, Mazu. Rest well." D'Molay got up, took a spear and stood near the doorway, keeping watch for any other threats. Looking out at the ruins in the darkness, he wondered why Mazu had been so hesitant to drink the nectar and what untold cost she might be enduring by doing so. Mazu was not one to reveal her personal secrets, so it was unlikely he would find out anytime soon.

Author Biographies

Ken St. Andre is a fantasy author, librarian and game designer, best known for his work with Tunnels & Trolls. He has been an active member of The Science Fiction and Fantasy Writers of America since 1989 and has had numerous fantasy and sci-fi stories published in collections and magazines. He also worked as a designer on the role-playing games Stormbringer, Monsters! Monsters!, and the computer game Wasteland. **www.trollhalla.com**

Wendall Brown was born in California and started one of the world's first computer game companies in 1981. He has written and/or produced dozens of fantasy and SF games, books, comics and screenplays including the Immortal series, Duelmasters, Hyborian War, Powerz, and many more. He currently resides in the Southwest where he continues to write for the screen, web and print. **www.powerzgame.com**

Robert Kassebaum lives in Escondido, California, where he currently works as a delivery driver. This is his first published fiction work. He lived in the City of the Gods as a librarian at the Great Library, which makes him eminently qualified to write about this mystical place.

Randy Lindsay: author, game designer, all around creative guy. At least, that's what it says on his business card. At home they call him the story-man because he comes up with stories about everything. Currently, his game design accomplishments outnumber his publishing credits, but he is working on changing that. His micro story *"He/She Said, She/He Said"* was published in Gentle Strength Quarterly and Twisted Entertainment posted his regular column on their website. Randy also has a blog for aspiring authors.

www.RandyLindsay.blogspot.com ◆ **www.randylindsay.net**

Wynn Mercere writes fantasy, horror, and historical fiction. In the '80s and '90s, Wynn did freelance work in the gaming and comics industries and was published under the names Debora Wykle and Debora Kerr. Many of these older titles are are still in print, including the gaming books Citybook VII: King's River Bridge and Maps 2: Places of Legend (published by Flying Buffalo, Inc.) In addition to the next volumes in the City of the Gods series, Wynn has two other novels in process. Practical Knack is a fantasy/adventure story set in early 20th Century America. Praesentia is a horror story set in ancient Rome. Wynn enjoys visiting historical sites, throwing theme parties, and collecting old U.S. coins. **www.wynnmercere.com**

Edgar Allan Poe (1809 – 1849) was an American author, poet, editor and literary critic, considered part of the American Romantic Movement. Best known for his tales of mystery and the macabre, Poe was one of the earliest American practitioners of the short story and is considered the inventor of the detective fiction and horror genres. He was the first well-known American writer to try to earn a living through writing alone, resulting in a financially difficult life and career

Jay Allen Sanford's fiction has appeared in publications like Twilight Zone Magazine, Cemetery Dance, In the Midnight Hour, and elsewhere. He co-created the comic book line Rock 'N' Roll Comics, among the top-selling independent comic books of the 1990s. His comic strip Rock Tales began in Rip Magazine and now runs in Spin. As a columnist and cartoonist for the San Diego Reader, the third most-circulated weekly newspaper in the U.S., he writes cover stories and maintains several columns, as well as drawing two weekly comic strips created specifically for the paper: Overheard in San Diego (debuted 1996) and Famous Former Neighbors (since 2004).

Bram Stoker (1847 – 1912) was an Irish novelist and short story writer, best known today for his 1897 Gothic novel Dracula. During his lifetime, he was better known as the personal assistant of actor Henry Irving and business manager of the Lyceum Theatre in London, which Irving owned. He also wrote Lair of the White Worm, twelve other novels and numerous short stories.

Jefferson P. Swycaffer is a San Diego resident, and a vigorous participant in organized fandom. He serves on several convention committees. He began writing fantasy, then switched to science fiction, for the "Concordat" series of novels from Avon Books, then switched back to fantasy again -- some people just can't make up their minds! -- writing "Warsprite" and "Web of Futures" for TSR. He is also a dedicated role playing gamer, a comics fan, and a pioneer in Furry fandom.

M. Scott Verne Co-creator of the City of the Gods world, M. Scott has co-written the CoG novels, the City of the Gods Map Pack, the Last Goddess Comic and this anthology. He spends a lot of his time researching the Knights Templar and regularly posts at Deadline Hollywood, with opinions on the latest Fantasy, Science fiction movies and TV shows.

Artist Biographies

Steve Crompton is the graphic designer for the City of the Gods products. He is also an illustrator best known for his work on Grimtooth's Traps, the Nuclear War Card Games and the Powerz Combat Game. His Graphics work on the City of the Gods Chapbook won the 2009 PIAZ (Printing Industries Arizona) Silver award for Design Excellence. Several other projects he's worked on have won Origins Game Industry Awards. See more of his work at **www.SteveCrompton.com**

Liz Danforth is an illustrator, writer, editor, and game developer best known for her artwork in ICE's Middle Earth books and card game, in many of the earlier Magic: the Gathering sets, and Tunnels & Trolls. She has worked as a game designer and developer on T&T, as a scenario designer for Interplay's Star Trek licenses, and many other projects. With a master's degree in library and information services, she works part time in libraries and blogged on games and gaming for almost three years for Library Journal as their pet games guru. At present, she is illustrating regularly, accepting private commissions, and working as concept artist, and world-development and concept advisor for Namasté Entertainment's amazing Storybricks project. Check out her art and blog at the Oakheart site, **www.lizdanforth.com.**

Gustave Doré (1832 – 1883) His first work was published in Paris in 1847. He worked as a caricaturist until gaining fame as an illustrator. In 1863 he was asked to illustrate the works of Lord Byron. This was followed by other work for British publishers including the illustrated Dore's English Bible (1865).   Dore's later work included Paradise Lost, King Arthur: The Idylls of the King and The Rime of the Ancient Mariner. His work also appeared in the Illustrated London News. Doré continued to illustrate books until his death on 23rd January 1883. His last book was the illustrated tales of Edgar Allen Poe.

David Roberts R.A. (1796 – 1864) a Scottish painter, especially known for a prolific series of detailed lithograph prints of Egypt and the Near East that he produced during the 1840s from sketches he made during long tours of the region (1838–1840). These, and his large oil paintings of similar subjects, made him a prominent Orientalist painter. He was elected as a Royal Academician in 1841.

Scribes Wanted!

Get your mythic story published in our next anthology

*T*he Council is seeking talented writers to chronicle new adventures in the City of the Gods. This is your chance to demonstrate your short story skills and have your work appear in the next Mythic Tales anthology.

AUDITION GUIDELINES

What is required

- Read City of the Gods: Forgotten and Mythic Tales.
- Familiarity with the Map Pack is not necessary, but recommended as it contains important details about the City's layout and locations.
- No previous publishing credits are required, but if you have them, please let us know.

What to send (2 Options)

- Send a 500 word writing sample featuring D'Molay encountering any god or goddess of your choice. The scene must take place in the City. This sample need not be part of a complete story that you wish to submit if you successfully complete the audition process and are invited to do so.
  OR:
- Send a description of the story you want to write for the next Anthology. The story should include at least one of the characters that appears in City of the Gods: Forgotten. A brief sample of some of your story writing would also be helpful.

Your reward

- All submissions that follow the rules will receive an exclusive City of the Gods souvenir crafted by co-creator Wynn Mercere.
- Some writers will be invited to submit a story for Mythic Tales 2 (to be published in 2013). Invitations will contain complete details on that process.
- Writers whose stories appear in Mythic Tales 2 will relieve a credit for writing the story and a contributor's copy of Mythic Tales 2, plus a special City of the Gods prize. It's a great way to get a publishing credit and visit the gods at the same time.

How to submit

- Email your audition to **info@wynnmercere.com** as a Microsoft Word .doc file or PDF attachment. Please include an email address you check regularly so that we can contact you.
- Deadline for auditions is September 30, 2012.

Art Credits

Art Credits contd.

More City of the Gods...

City of the Gods Map Pack

Usable with any role-playing system, the Map Pack includes: 11 x 17 full color detailed map of the City of the Gods. 20 page book that describes over 105 places in the city, details on the world of the Gods and 54 scenarios the GM can use to incorporate his existing game into the City of the Gods. Full color map of the realms of the Gods. 18 full color NPC cards of gods and citizens from the City. Two 32 page signed City of the Gods Comics. Plus a booklet with a chapter from the first City of the Gods novel. $19.95

The Last Goddess #1 - City of the Gods Universe

The Gods left Earth long ago - or did they? At Dunwich Asylum, two evil gods secretly attempt to rebuild their powers and gain new converts on Earth. One remaining goddess of the light is reborn to try and thwart them, but is it already too late? Can this naked, beautiful and confused woman rediscover her god-hood and stop the coming of a reign of evil that would make Earth a living Hell? Can she adapt to the modern world after being dead for over a thousand years? Gorgeous art throughout! Also includes additional bonus material. **This comic is for mature readers.** By M.Scott Verne & Wynn Mercere. $7.95

City of the Gods: Guardian

This second book in the series continues the adventures of D'Molay and Mazu as they hunt for Circe, honoring the pledge they made to Glaucus. The search causes them to delve deeper into the hidden mysteries surrounding the City of the Gods. By M.Scott Verne & Wynn Mercere. $18.95 (Due out in late 2012)

Check our website at **www.cityofthegods.com**
for the latest news and info.

**You can also order directly from
Opus Graphics - PO Box 2018, Scottsdale, AZ 85252.
Send check or money order** (prices include shipping in the US)